Pearls
on a
Broken String

Pearls On a Broken String

Valerie Cox

Print ISBN: 978-1-54390-263-1

eBook ISBN: 978-1-54390-264-8

All Scripture quotations, unless otherwise indicated, are taken from the Holy Bible, New International Version®, NIV®. Copyright ©1973, 1978, 1984, 2011 by Biblica, Inc.™ Used by permission of Zondervan. All rights reserved worldwide. www. zondervan.com The "NIV" and "New International Version" are trademarks registered in the United States Patent and Trademark Office by Biblica, Inc.™

Permission from Vineyard Music to publish song lyrics, "Come Now Is the Time to Worship"

for my nieces and nephews
Jordan, James, Audra, Zane, Nathan, and Julia...

to all my *Grace Notes* gals...

to all my students throughout the years who have wanted to read
this book...

and if you hold this book in your hands,

may you know the joy of believing.

Ava's Top Ten—South Africa

Mug and Bean
Cape of Good Hope
Meeting Jessie
Pearl Necklace!
Mercy Ships' tour
Rainbow from Lion's Head
Christmas morning with Grandpa and Grandma
Cape Town Baptist Church
Camps Bay picnic
Kirstenbosch

CHAPTER 1

"Come on. Sit in my lap," Torin coaxed. "Just for a minute. Or don't you trust me?"

The question hung unanswered in the thick morning fog. Ava was still trying to figure this guy out. What exactly did he expect? Her heart still raced from the trust fall he'd challenged her to. Ava replayed the scene in her mind while Torin waited on her answer.

"On the count of three, okay?" she heard Torin say. "One, two..."

Ava wanted to trust him.

"Three."

She let herself fall backward, eyes squeezed shut, right into Torin's strong arms. It was a good feeling to be caught.

And now Torin wanted to know if she'd sit in his lap.

"Let's keep going," Ava answered quickly, pulling her dark brown hair back with a hair tie and flipping her purple hoodie over her head. An early October cool front chilled the air. Torin scooted closer to her on the bench they'd discovered about a quarter mile down the trail and wrapped his arm around her shivering shoulders. His arms were so strong.

"I thought we were supposed to be jogging, not sitting here on a bench," Ava teased, trying to ease the tension she felt. She bent over to empty an imaginary pebble from her shoe and pulled her laces tighter. Torin pulled her back to him.

"We *did* jog," Torin answered. Besides, we're just taking a quick break."

"Two minutes? That's hardly a jog. Now come on!" Ava jumped to her feet, stepping playfully past Torin to continue their first training run.

Torin clutched her wrist firmly in his hand before she could pass him.

"Come on, Torin. Let's jog. The 5K is in two weeks," she said, pulling gently. "Let go, please." She heard the seriousness in her own voice, but he wasn't letting go. The seconds slipped into the fog. "You're supposed to be helping me get in shape, silly," she teased.

Ava's secret senior crush was no longer a secret now that Torin had broken up with Emily, a girl he'd started dating in August. Ava barely knew either one of them, since Emily was a sophomore and Torin had only come to Wilson High last year.

Ever since last week, when Torin had promised Ava he'd help her place in the 5K, every day had felt a blue-sky summer day. But the blue-sky feeling was quickly being swallowed by the fog, along with her hope of romance. She knew instinctively—this wasn't it.

"I thought we'd just stop for a minute," he said, not loosening the grip on her wrist. "You trust me, right?" He didn't even sound winded. They'd only jogged from the trail head at Forest Creek to the bridge in Rock Creek Park, but she was breathing full and strong. She felt trapped. Ava hoped another jogger or two would pass by, but perhaps Torin had chosen a less-traveled trail on purpose.

"Be careful!" Ava's dad had called from the front porch when they'd left her house on foot. "Stay on the busy trails!"

Her dad's warnings broke through the fog.

"Please let go. I mean it." She said it a little louder this time and she felt the heavy thud of her heart, warning her to flee.

"Ava," he said sweetly. "Don't you trust me?"

"Of course I trust you." She lied. "Just let me go, okay? I have to go the bathroom. Let's jog back to the trail head before we get too far from my house." Ava tried to pull away again, but she sensed his power. Why wasn't he letting go?

"I'll let you go if…"

"Hey, let her go!" came a threat from somewhere along the woodsy path.

Torin let go. Ava saw the fleeting look of panic on his face give way to a steely-eyed glare. "You're not worth it anyway. Tell anyone about this and you'll regret it," he hissed through clenched teeth.

He jogged further into the park, appearing calm, but Ava hoped he'd been sufficiently terrified. He wouldn't want anyone at school to find out about this outing. Ava didn't want word to get out either. She feared he was capable of far worse. Before he rounded the curve, he hollered back, "Thanks for jogging with me, Ava! See you at school."

"Jerk!" Ava muttered. *What a lame cover up.* Heart beating, legs shaking, trying desperately to regain her composure, she glanced quickly in the direction from which the voice had come, but only the rustle of dying leaves answered her. She was too afraid to call out. No one came forward. Was she alone? Was someone watching her?

You're not worth it anyway. The suffocating words descended from the fog.

With all her will, she sprinted up the trail towards home. She would stay outside until her face no longer betrayed her panic.

You're not worth it anyway. The words stung her heart, but no one would ever know. *Of course I'm worth it.*

*　*　*

Ava hit the alarm clock on Monday morning and rolled over to face the window, staring out at the small, fenced yard, hemmed with azaleas and rhododendrons that had long quit blooming. Her dying flower garden, a rewarding summer project, tried to be brave in the last sunny days as winter approached.

Ava felt her life was rather like that yard, small and protected. Safe. Mostly safe. Saturday hadn't been too safe. The last thing she wanted to do was go to school. She was actually afraid of Torin now, and she didn't know how things would go when they saw each other again. How had things gone so wrong?

She threw on her most comfy jeans with a long-sleeved gray T-shirt and looked in the mirror. Was she pretty? Ava only cared that her clothes were comfortable. Perhaps she should care more. Her mom was always telling her she was beautiful and that she should wear clothes that would bring out that beauty. Wasn't she right? Her stubborn hair never held a curl. Why did she even try? She reached for a hair band and swept her hair into a ponytail. Today, she just wanted to blend into the crowd.

She applied some creamy beige powder to her smooth, olive complexion. A little blush, a little bronze eye shadow to complement her chocolate brown eyes, a few sweeps of mascara, and little vanilla mint lip gloss—that was more than enough. It took less than five minutes.

Heading downstairs to the kitchen, she could barely finish the scrambled eggs and bacon her dad made her every Monday morning as his tradition to start the week off right, but she didn't disappoint him.

"See ya later, Dad. Thanks for breakfast!" She tried to sound cheerful as she headed out the door for Wilson High.

"You're welcome, Ava. You're absolutely beautiful, you know."

First period. Ava slunk into her seat, two behind Torin's, and kept her eyes glued to her pre-cal textbook. She pulled out her homework and erased a problem she *knew* was correct, just to look busy. She definitely didn't want to answer anyone's questions.

"So, Ava," whispered Miranda, who'd slipped into the seat behind her, "I overheard Torin telling some guys this morning that he was going to ask Kathy Freeman to the homecoming dance. I thought he was going to ask you. Didn't you two go running Saturday?"

"Huh?" Ava said, looking up from her papers. "Oh, yeah. We went running, but I just don't think I'm too interested in him. Don't worry. It's mutual. And I...really don't want to talk about it now, Miranda. You know?" She pointed towards Torin's empty seat. She dreaded the moment he'd walk in.

At this point, Ava was sure that she would just skip the homecoming dance in two weeks. Too much drama. Life would be much simpler just sticking to movie and mall dates with Miranda. *Yeah, I'll just spend next weekend with her—if she doesn't have plans. That will be much safer.*

CHAPTER 2

The bell rang and Ava slipped out of her journalism class, taking the long route to the cafeteria to avoid running into Torin. It had been a week since he'd left her on the trail.

That's when she saw him. Not Torin. No. Someone else. *He must be new here.* Just one glance, one look, and she knew that there was something different about this guy. They passed each other and their eyes met briefly. She smiled without thinking, as if to say hello. He smiled back. And she spent the rest of the day figuring out a way to meet this new guy "naturally."

"Can I leave early for lunch?" she asked Mr. Davis the next day, five minutes before the lunch bell. "I really have to go to the bathroom. It's an emergency. Please?"

Mr. Davis let her go, no questions asked. Ava was thankful for her good reputation. She rushed to the bathroom to keep up appearances, and then planted herself at the edge of the Commons area and waited for the bell to ring. Sure enough, she spotted him. He was the last one out of Mrs. Lamin's English class. When he passed by, she followed him as inconspicuously as possible.

Once in the cafeteria line, a first for her, she noticed the necklace he was wearing—a couple of leather straps holding a tarnished-looking bow and arrow, a few golden-colored rings, and a cross. When he turned her way again, Ava took the chance. It was now or never.

"That's a cool necklace," Ava heard herself say.

"Thank you. I got it in Korea," the stranger said. "By the way, my name's Michael." Michael stuck out his hand and Ava shook it. Ava's hunch had been right. Already, this guy was so different.

"Ava," she said, and all at once, she realized didn't have anything to keep this conversation going. *Great.*

"Ava? Hmmm…" His kind eyes narrowed and he tilted his head as if he were recalling anyone else he'd known by that name. "*Very* nice to meet you." He hesitated. "You already sitting with someone? You're welcome to join me."

Ava hadn't anticipated this. What *had* she expected? Maybe just a conversation. Nothing more. Would Miranda be waiting on her?

"Sure, I'll eat with you." She grasped for words and asked the obvious. "You're new here, right?"

"Yes, indeed. This is my second day. My dad finished up a job in Korea, so we're back here in D.C. for a while."

"Korea? What was he doing in Korea?"

"He teaches English, for one thing," Michael told her, "but…. we came home because my grandma has cancer. My dad's going to stay with her through the treatment. It's an aggressive cancer, but it's curable."

"Oh, I'm so sorry."

"Yeah, it's tough. My dad is an only child. And my grandpa died when my dad was quite young—in Viet Nam. My grandma never remarried, and she lives alone. I'm sorry. I didn't mean to go into all these details, it's just…"

"No, no. Don't apologize," Ava interrupted. "It's just… what?"

"It's just that it's been on my mind so much," Michael told her.

"So, how long will you be here at Wilson High?" Ava asked, picking up a tray and fumbling for a small bottle of water.

"Probably the rest of the year. My dad's not quite sure. He wants to get back, but not until my grandma is better."

"What about your mom? Is she…."

"Ah, it's just me and my dad." Michael interrupted her. He led her to a table on the far side of the cafeteria. With his tray in one hand, he pulled out a chair and motioned for her to sit down.

"Do you graduate this year?" Ava thought quickly of another question to patch the delicate break in conversation.

"Yes, if all my credits transfer, which they should," he said.

"I graduate this year, too." Ava smiled. Secretly, she felt proud of her intuition about this guy. He was definitely not like Torin. "So what are your plans after high school?"

"I'm not exactly sure. College definitely, and then maybe something involving international negotiations." Michael smiled, raising his eyebrows as if he were plotting a secret life as a spy. "You?"

Ava told him all about her aspirations to become a journalist and how she loved the idea of traveling and writing. He asked her how she'd become interested in that field, and for the next fifteen minutes, he listened and asked more questions as she shared.

Ava regretted not asking *him* more questions that day, because the next day, Miranda wanted her back at her usual table, not "flirting" with some new guy, who, it was already rumored, was a little "off."

"Seriously, Ava. What do you see in that guy? He's so not as cute as Torin," Miranda commented after their first conversation at lunch.

"Torin? Torin's history," Ava answered. That's all she ever answered to anyone when anyone cared to ask. And she vowed that was all she would ever answer.

But that day at lunch with Michael, she sensed she could tell him anything. Why was that? How could that happen with a complete stranger?

"Torin might be a jerk, but that guy you're talking to? I work in the office, and he turned in a form to request permission to start a Christian group before school. And that was just yesterday, his first day here." Miranda rolled her eyes and sighed. "Now what do you think of him?" Miranda added.

Ava, disappointed by this revelation, knew that Michael was definitely no longer an option, but she consoled herself in her previous decision to just stick with her girlfriends. Michael was one of *those* people who trusted in an unseen, divine power. She knew she'd never be able to date someone like that. And, as a matter of course, she had practically ignored him for another month after Miranda broke the news to her.

Until November sixteenth, to be exact. She had been in the hallway, going from pre-cal to history.

"Hey, Ava!" Torin had caught up with her and sounded friendly and warm. That horrid October Saturday had come and gone and they hadn't spoken a word since. Ava had done everything she could to avoid him. She was becoming an expert at avoiding things.

Torin looked contrite standing there with his two buddies. For a split second, Ava thought he might apologize. Then he blurted out, "Wanna go jogging with me again?" with a smirk on his face. Torin's buddies doubled over in laughter, slapping each other on the back. Ava felt her face flush as she stood there in shock.

Out of nowhere, a tall, unassuming boy stepped between her and Torin. He raised his hands, palms forward, toward Torin. "Hey, leave her alone. For the second time." His voice was stern and unwavering.

"Who's he?" Torin asked, addressing Ava, clearly dazed that anyone would confront him and obviously confused by this stranger's cryptic comment. "Your new boyfriend?" His mocking tone pierced her heart.

"I don't even know him!" The words hadn't left her lips before she wished she could take them back. Someone had come to her rescue, and she denied she'd ever even talked to him before. Of course she knew Michael. His dad worked in Korea. His grandma had cancer. But Miranda had warned her, and Ava knew it was best not to get involved.

Before she could take her words back, Michael was far down the hall. Ava wondered what he thought of her now, if he even cared that she hadn't talked to him since they'd met. He'd been so kind that day at lunch, and then she'd totally abandoned him and gone back to eating lunch with her own crowd. He didn't seem to mind. He never made a point to come talk to her either. They had exchanged a few polite smiles in the hallway. That was all.

Just before lunch, in her journalism class, Ava scribbled a note to Michael. She slipped it to him as he waited in the cafeteria line, and then she found Miranda sitting by herself. The routine crowd would be there soon enough with their usual lunch time chatter, but Ava's mind was on the words she'd written to Michael.

Hi Michael,

    I'm really sorry that I said I didn't know you. The words just came out before I could even think. I was so humiliated. Thanks for sticking up for me. But I have one question. Why did you tell Torin to leave me alone—for the second time? Again, I'm so sorry. Please forgive me. Let's eat lunch again?

—Ava

During lunch, Ava cast her eyes across the Commons to try to catch Michael's reaction. Pen in hand, between bites, he scribbled something on the paper she'd given him.

Within a few minutes, Michael had walked over and handed her the note he'd written. Ava brushed off Miranda's insensitive remarks and tucked the note in her purse to read when she was alone.

"Ava." Miranda waved her hands in front of Ava's face. "Hey, stop looking over there. What's going on with you? What did that guy give you?"

"His name is *Michael*, Miranda."

"Ok, sorry. What did *Michael* give you?" Miranda seemed irritated.

"You said something to Torin, didn't you?" Ava demanded the truth from Miranda. "I told you not to worry about it. To just drop it. I don't even know why I told you."

"Look, he's not going to treat you like that and get away with it," Miranda insisted.

Ava glared back. "I just wanted you to stop bugging me about him. I didn't want you to try to fix things. Now you've just made them worse." Ava slumped in her chair, arms crossed. "I told you not to tell anyone, and that included him. I thought we were supposed to be best friends. How am I supposed to trust you now? He humiliated me in the hallway." Ava kept her voice low so no one would hear.

"What? How? What happened?" Miranda looked remorseful enough. Ava could tell she wanted to hear the whole story in dramatic detail.

"But you know who came to my rescue?" Ava asked her.

"To your rescue?"

"Yeah. To my rescue. You know what? I don't think you deserve to know. I gotta go to the bathroom. But I'll probably end up telling you later anyway." Ava headed for the restroom, clutching her purse, eager to read Michael's response.

The bathroom stall provided the privacy she needed as she pulled out the note Michael had returned.

Dear Ava,

It's quite alright. No worries. I very much enjoyed meeting you last month. And when you introduced yourself, your name sounded so familiar. It wasn't until I saw that guy teasing you yesterday in the hallway, that I put things together. That was you on the trail that day. I apologize if I made you uncomfortable, but I just can't stand by when guys treat girls with no respect.

Sincerely,
Michael

P.S. You can eat lunch with me and Ben anytime.

Ava couldn't believe it. *Michael* was the one who had hollered for Torin to let her go on the trail? *How can that be? Maybe he lives close to Rock Creek Park, too. What does he think of me now?*

That day, Ava made a decision. *Who cares what Miranda thinks.*

The following day when the bell rang for lunch, she headed straight for Michael's table. "Can I eat lunch with you two today?" Ava asked.

Michael sat with Ben—a boy Ava had often seen reading by himself. "Of course. You're welcome here," Michael said.

Ava sat down. No words needed to be said. He'd come to her rescue twice. It was a mystery how Michael had happened to be in the right place at the right time, but he had.

"Hey, Ava. Ben and I were just talking about Christian Student Fellowship. We've got permission to start the group, but not until January. We were just talking about the meetings, and we're inviting people. You interested?"

"Well, I…" Ava didn't want to say no right away. She felt like she couldn't do that to Michael, not after what he'd done for her. "I just may show up. You never know. When will you meet?"

"Wednesday mornings, 7:30," Ben said. "It'll be fun."

Fun? Ava had second thoughts. *I should just tell them the truth.* "I'm not exactly a Christian," she blurted out, feeling relieved. "I don't…like… believe in God or anything, and so it would be silly for me to try to come."

"Not silly at all," Michael said. "You're welcome to come, whether you believe in God or not. You can just see what it's all about. Ask questions…"

"That would be a little… weird," Ava admitted.

"If you ask questions, and seek answers, you just might discover some truth. But if you never ask and never seek…" Michael left his sentence unfinished.

"If you want to know if God exists, just ask him, and see what happens. I'm confident He won't let you down if you truly seek Him," Ben added, almost robotically.

It sounded so strange to hear these things. Ava had never really talked to Christians about God. She decided to change the subject. Maybe they could still be friends.

"How's your grandma doing?" she asked.

"Oh, thanks for asking. She's having a hard time, but she's strong. She's always had a positive outlook on life, no matter what's going on."

"I'm glad. I know that must be hard." Ava wanted desperately to make up for being thoughtless and cruel to Michael the day before.

"Doing anything exciting for Christmas break?" Ava changed the subject again.

"Nah, not necessarily," Michael told her. "Dad is pretty busy helping my grandma. We'll probably do a few touristy things in D.C. and just keep helping my grandma with her doctors' appointments and errands. What about you?"

"Glad you asked. My mom and dad and I are going to South Africa for Christmas to visit my grandparents. I haven't seen them in forever, since I was about four. How's that for exciting?"

"Very. Hey, I collect postcards," Michael volunteered. "I have about fifty from different places. I guess it all started with my aunt sending me postcards from all her travels, and I just started collecting them. So when I visit a new place, I buy a postcard, write a memory on the back, and add it to a little wooden box I made when I was a kid."

"That's so cool." Ava paused, imagining where all the postcards were from and wishing she could read them. "I'll help you build your collection. I'll send you a postcard from South Africa," Ava promised. "I sure will."

CHAPTER 3

December 18, 2005 (Sunday)

Dear Michael,

I'm not planning on giving you this letter, but I thought I'd write to you anyway. We're finally on the way to South Africa! Very excited to see Grandma and Grandpa Cotzee. Ready to be off this flight already. But it's amazing how beautiful the sky is from up here!! The sun is rising up through a huge sea of clouds, and I'm trying to imagine you flying over Iceland and realizing that Iceland is green and Greenland is icy. Amusing! So, are you finding anything fun to do over winter break? Thanks for inviting me to sit with you at lunch—after all that happened. I'm honestly very sorry. All I can say is thank you. You seem so mysterious. What secrets are you hiding? And I've been meaning to ask you more about Korea.

So you're really inviting me to that group you're starting up? I don't think you'd invite me if you only knew me and my family. What will the meeting be like, anyway? What's the point? I mean, seems like an unanswerable question, I suppose, but...how can anyone be so sure God exists? My grandpa says religion is just something people created to explain why the sun comes up. Just the other day, the Georgetown Times *published another one of his editorials. He argued that the rights of atheists are being ignored, and he cited a complaint by a student who was offended because of a prayer at her graduation. He has some good points. But seriously, does God exist? How can anyone really know? Isn't there some kind of...*

*   *   *

"Ham or sausage croissant?" The flight attendant asked politely.

"Ham, please," Ava told her. Quickly, she shoved her journal into her lap bag and pulled down the tray table, suddenly aware

VALERIE COX

of her rumbling stomach. She was hungrier than she realized. The flight from D.C. to London was 7 hours 19 minutes according to her ticket, and since the flight had departed at 9:46 P.M., she hadn't eaten in a while. She hadn't slept much either. The other passengers were beginning to stir after what seemed to Ava a very restless night. What time was it anyway, way above the Atlantic, racing toward London? Pressing a button on the screen of the seat in front of her, she found the *local time at destination* to be six hours ahead of D.C., which meant they'd arrive in London at 10:05 A.M. They'd have a long layover until their next flight departed for South Africa at 9:00 P.M. that night.

Ava looked forward to being in London for those ten hours or so, because her mom and dad had said they could leave the airport and eat lunch by the Thames River. Maybe they would even ride the London Eye, a huge Ferris wheel located along the banks. Ava predicted that, after all the traveling, she'd wake up in the middle of the night at her grandma's house in Cape Town and not be able to sleep because her body clock was still on D.C. time or London time, or somewhere-in-between time.

A spunky young woman with curly auburn hair sat next to her, thoroughly caught up in a book. Ava approved completely. She knew the feeling of being lost in a good book, and that was exactly why they hadn't yet struck up a conversation.

"What's your destination?" the lady asked unexpectedly, closing her book with a snap and a sigh. Startled, Ava stammered, "Uhm... Cape Town."

"Wonderful! That's where I'm from. I'm assuming you're going to spend Christmas there? Do you have family there?" The woman came alive with questions.

"Yes. My mom is from there originally, but she came to the States when she was seventeen." Ava kicked the bottom of the seat in front of her where her mom was sitting. She wasn't going to tell a perfect stranger that her mom had been chasing a guy when she moved to Washington D.C., but she wouldn't let her mom forget that she knew.

— 14 —

"My grandma and grandpa still live in Cape Town, but the last time I visited them was, let's see, about thirteen years ago when I was four. Ava paused. "And you? What brought you to the States?"

"Ah. Good question. I'm studying business at Southeastern in D.C.," she said, taking a bite of her croissant.

"Really? My grandpa's a history professor there."

"Ah, how wonderful. But I probably wouldn't know your grandpa. I don't know any of the history professors there." The woman marked her place in her book. "Are you going to visit any special sites while you're in Cape Town?"

"Oh, yes. My grandma has it all planned out. My birthday is next week, so I'm sure she has a few surprises. I'll be eighteen." Reaching between the seats, Ava tapped her mom's shoulder. "Hey, Mom. Where are some of the places we'll visit?"

Mrs. Zinfield turned awkwardly and spoke through the seats. "Let's see. Boulder's Beach, Kirstenbosch, Table Mountain, Cape Point. At least, we hope so."

"I don't remember much from my last visit," Ava told the woman.

"You'll find South Africa to be very beautiful—just like a dream, some parts." The young woman grew solemn. "Only, unfortunately, there are some nightmares in the dream if you look deeply into the landscape of our past. So don't look too deeply. Just look for the beauty."

Ava thought the woman sounded like a poet. Why, then, was she studying business? They both lapsed into silence and Ava recalled the strange dream she'd had the night before. The dream was vivid and real, like so many of her dreams. She was in the library with some friends and they were talking, perhaps giving her advice, when she noticed a white dress shoe with sparkly sequins in the trash can. She pulled the shoe out and checked the size. Size seven. Her exact size. Her friends had kept on talking, seeming not to notice.

Do dreams really have meanings?

Don't look too deeply. Just look for the beauty. The woman's words ricocheted in her mind.

Jarred back to reality by sudden turbulence, Ava clutched her bag and steadied the cranberry juice on her tray table.

The spunky woman had opened her book again. Curious, Ava ventured to interrupt the woman's reverie. "So what are you reading?" Perhaps she could learn more valuable insights from this native South African while she had the opportunity. Perhaps she could discover something she needed to know, although she couldn't even imagine what that might be.

"It's called the *No. 1 Ladies' Detective Agency*. It's a series of books, actually. Haven't you heard of them? They're quite delightful. The detective, a lady, solves the most mysterious cases."

"Like what?" Ava asked, thinking of the unsolved mysteries of her own life. *Does or does not God exist, for example. And why doesn't my mother ever want to talk about my biological South African grandfather?*

"Oh, you'd probably love these books," the stranger recommended, not answering her question. "By the way, my name is Stefanie."

"I'm Ava. Nice to meet you, Stefanie."

Maybe Stefanie had seen Ava's library book from school by Tamora Pierce. On the front cover was a girl warrior, defending invisible lands almost single-handedly. "Let's see. The detective is a woman, for one thing. She's not your typical detective, that is. For instance, her only possessions include two desks, two chairs, a little white van, a telephone, a teapot, three teacups, and an old typewriter. And she solves cases that are so ordinary—not at all like American detective stories. For example, right now, she's trying to figure out whether or not a young Indian girl has a boyfriend."

"That *does* sound interesting," Ava admitted. She thought about Michael. Michael was just a boy "space" friend, however.

"You should check one out sometime. She's involved in so many very ordinary cases that most people might consider not worth their time. But she's so intuitive, so intelligent in how she solves the cases. Definitely a page-turner."

"Ok, I'll try to check one out soon," Ava said. She pulled her journal out of her lap bag and made a note in the margin. She saw her unfinished sentence. She tried to recall what she had intended to write. *Isn't there some kind of... some kind of...*

She remembered and, taking her pen, finished her thought. *Some kind of evidence for things like this???*

The young woman had turned back to her book, and Ava didn't want to interrupt again. Besides, she felt satisfied by this new book recommendation.

Ava's thoughts flashed back to earlier that day. She and her mom and dad had taken a taxi to the airport, and barreling through the streets of D.C., she had seen something she'd never seen before. It was a public bus. That was the ordinary part. But there on the side, in big bold letters, a question had jumped out at her: *"Why believe in a god? Just be good for goodness' sake."*

Ordinarily, Ava might not have given a question like this a second thought. Perhaps it was Michael's invitation to the Christian club that had forced her to stop and think. She had fond memories of believing in Santa Claus, leaving Snickerdoodle cookies and a glass of milk on a Christmas-tree-shaped tray next to the fireplace for him to find when he dropped off her new pink bicycle.

The familiar Christmas tune jostled around in her head. She thought of her grandpa's editorial, and she thought of her big mysteries to solve, and she thought of the lady detective in Africa, wondering how she'd crack the case of the Indian girl with the possible boyfriend. She imagined calling her up for a little advice. After Torin, she had thought she would leave boys alone for the rest of her life.

But then there was Michael. Peering out the window, down at the vast expanse she knew was ocean, she could see his blue-green eyes. They were so kind. Somehow, when she was around him, she could truly believe that she was worthy. She tried to imagine what made him believe there was a God. She closed her eyes and attempted to get some sleep as the massive 747, a speck in the sky, raced closer to

London, to Africa, and new adventures to be had, but all she could do was replay the events of the last few months. Where did it all begin?

CHAPTER 4

"How was the flight?" Grandma Coetzee asked with a tone of sincere inquiry.

"Too long," Ava groaned. "I think I need a nap."

"Try your very best to stay awake until bedtime tonight. You'll sleep better and won't experience too much jet lag. If all goes as planned, we'll begin our adventures tomorrow," Grandma added, without a hint of hurry. "Meanwhile, I have some brunch ready for us out on the patio."

Ava sat listening to her parents catch up with a grandma she barely knew. The distance was great. People were busy. But now, instead of a ten-year-old, still-life photo sitting on the piano, her grandmother came to life, speaking crisply and energetically in that distinct South African accent, her hair now completely gray. She asked Ava every conceivable question. *How's school? Where will you go to college? What's your best class in school? Do you have any hobbies? Do you have a boyfriend?* Yes, there was always *that* question.

It was obvious that there was pent up frustration between her mom and her grandma. Certain glances and sighs confirmed this to be true. But Ava still didn't know why. Yet another mystery. She supposed there were always such glances and sighs between parents and their adult children. She'd observed a similar tension between her dad and his parents from time to time.

Around noon, Grandma suggested they all take a trip to the Victoria Wharf for some extravagant purchases at the spacious, nothing-lacking shopping mall. Ava couldn't hide her astonishment. She hadn't pictured big, fancy shopping malls in South Africa.

"And after you ladies are tired of shopping, I'll treat everyone to dessert at Mug and Bean," Grandpa Coetzee suggested. Famous for its Arabica coffee and giant muffins and delicious cakes, Mugg and Bean earned an immediate spot on Ava's top-ten list of favorite places in South Africa as the chocolate icing melted in her mouth.

But it was the beginning of the trip. Who knew if her list would be crowded out by adventures yet to be had.

Ava reflected on whether being in a different country could change a person. That night as she lay in bed, she felt a strange yet peaceful sense of something stirring in her soul.

The next day Ava and her parents zipped through Cape Town's streets with Grandma and Grandpa Coetzee. First stop—Table Mountain, appropriately named because it literally resembled a table, flat on top. Ava had never experienced anything quite like the giant sentinel, towering above the V&A Waterfront, keeping faithful watch over the city. The port was teeming with ships bobbing, buildings dancing, and colors splashing across the blue sky. Clouds spilled over the top of the great mountain, covering it like a giant tablecloth, a postcard-perfect scene. *How beautiful!* Below the cloud-breathing giant, Ava's heart danced with adventures soon to come.

"There's Devil's Peak to the East and Lion's Head to the West," Grandpa Coetzee said with an air of authority as they drove through the city toward the base of the mountain. "And the Devil and old pirate Van Hunks are trying to out-smoke each other again."

"What?" Ava asked, raising her eyebrows.

"Oh, it's just an old legend, that when you see those clouds spilling over the mountain, the Devil and a pirate are having a smoking contest," Grandma said. "If it doesn't clear up soon, we won't be going to the top today."

Grandma Coetzee pointed out a tiny raised spot at the far end of the mountain. "And that's Table Mountain's cable-car station. Step onto that cable car, and you'll be at the top in five minutes. Such a spectacular view. Ava, your mother and dad were engaged at the top of that mountain."

Ava knew the story well, but hearing it again, her thoughts turned to her biological grandfather, whom no one seemed willing to talk about. He had died before she was born, and that's about all Mom would say. Deciding there was no better time, she bravely asked, "Where were you and Grandfather engaged? Grandpa Amery,

I mean." She took a deep breath and held it, letting it out slowly. How had she been so brave to ask?

Ava had never met the tall, strong grandfather she'd seen in scrapbooks and photo frames. One picture, in particular, she remembered vividly now. The sun setting behind him, and Table Mountain a silhouette, her biological grandfather was holding open an oyster shell with a pearl inside, barely visible. His smile seemed to be just for her, Ava thought.

"Ah, yes. Grandpa Avery. Your grandfather and I met at church," Grandma Coetzee said in a lovely South African accent.

Ava's eyes grew wide, although she tried to hide her bewilderment at this new revelation. Ava's mom sighed, clearly irritated that Grandma Coetzee had shared this bit of information and that Ava had dared bring up the fragile past.

"Can I not tell my granddaughter where I met her grandfather? That's all I'm doing," Grandma Coetzee said calmly.

Why are they keeping this a secret from me? What could possibly be so terrible? I hate this tension. I shouldn't have brought it up. But I want answers. People should TALK about things. Ava realized she was clenching her teeth. She wanted to know more about the church comment.

Sensing her frustration, Mrs. Zinfield reassured her daughter, but Ava didn't miss the sarcasm. "I'm sure Grandma will tell you all you want to know."

Although Ava wasn't completely ignorant, so much of her mom's past was a closed book. Her dad's side of the family held fewer secrets. Dad's roots were obvious. He'd grown up the son of history professor who was adamantly opposed to all talk of religion—unless he was speaking against it. That was certain. Grandpa's editorial in the *Washington Post* had been one of many derailing religion. Ava had known his position for a long time, and Dad was no less vocal. She'd heard him say countless times as they watched the news and something religious was aired, "I can't believe so many people can be deluded by a bunch of superstitions. I just don't get it."

Ava's mom, who had lost most of her accent after having lived in the States for twenty years, would just scrunch her eyebrows and say, "Now don't be so hard on them, honey."

Them. The religious people. The people who believed in God. The people who believed in superstitions and trusted in something they couldn't even see. Something they couldn't even prove. But why had Mom told Dad not to be so hard on them? Was it because her own mom and dad met in church? Maybe this explains Mom's unpredictable behavior.

The tension in the car eased when Grandpa pulled onto Tafelberg Road and parked. From here, they took a taxi to the Lower Cable Station, and as everyone boarded the spacious cable car, the little remaining tension was replaced by the grandeur and beauty of adventure. They were going to the top after all. The clouds were clearing.

Though it was December, and snow blanketed neighborhoods in D. C., the people of South Africa enjoyed a sunny, summer day. At peak season, the cable car was filled to capacity. Sixty-five adventure seekers ascended magically and effortlessly into the sky, and Ava jostled for a position next to one of the dozen or so huge windows. The cable car spun around slowly, a full three-hundred and sixty degrees, allowing all the passengers to glimpse the beautiful gorge, the rocky cliffs, and the waterfront down below, which grew smaller and smaller every second as they climbed higher and higher.

At the top, the group unloaded and headed in all directions, the most popular direction towards the gift shops and cafes. Grandpa Coetzee put his hand on Ava's shoulder. "Let's head this direction," he said. They all followed the trail that led to "The City Bowl" view. The vista took Ava's breath away. On the far left, Lion's Head jutted up toward the sky, but from the top of Table Mountain, it looked like only a small volcano without a hole in the top.

Huge gray boulders cascaded down the mountain toward a barren, green stretch of land that gave way to the sprawling city, hugging the Atlantic in a horseshoe-shaped embrace. On the far right, Devil's Peak commanded attention.

And so the city lay, Ava observed, between Lion's Head and Devil's Peak.

"Ava," Grandpa Coetzee said, pointing out toward the water. "See that island way out there in the distance? Do you know what island that is?"

"Robben Island?" Ava said, hoping she was right. "Tell me more about it. Isn't that where Nelson Mandela was sent?"

"Yes, that's right," he said.

Ava's mom, who had followed along in silence as they had walked toward the City Bowl, unexpectedly broke in. "Your Grandpa Amery, my dad, died fighting against apartheid. I was only seven, Ava." Mrs. Zinfield stared at the tiny dot that was Robben Island. "He was on his way to a gathering of people who were trying to find answers. And he was killed in a car accident."

"I was never convinced it was an accident," Grandma Coetzee broke in. "Not at all. My husband was a fighter. People wanted him stopped. That island is such a reminder to me of all he stood for."

Ava's heart thudded with the cruel truth being revealed. She'd never heard her mom mention anything like this before.

Her mom continued, "Every day for years growing up, I pretended he was there on that island in prison instead of..." Ava saw the tears welling up in her mother's eyes.

It seemed a relief for Ava's mom and grandma to disclose that secret, and Ava realized they'd likely planned it the way they took turns. Ava had always assumed there was knowledge which was held back from her, knowledge too painful for her to be burdened with as a child. But she was no longer a child. She'd already seen so much ugliness in the world, but none so close to her own family.

So that's what happened to my real grandpa? Not only was he a church-goer, but he was fighting apartheid, too, and died doing so? Ava's thoughts were spinning from Michael's invitation, to Mom and Grandma's sudden confession, to the picture of Grandpa Amery holding the oyster with the pearl inside. Whenever Ava had asked about that picture, her mom had only responded, "That's my dad, Sweetie. Your Grandpa Amery. I wish you could have known him."

Ava wished so, too—very much so. She'd never thought to ask how Grandpa Coetzee had come into the picture, but now she wanted to know.

Devil's Peak loomed larger now. "What a name for a mountain overlooking an infamous prison," Ava thought aloud.

"Yes," said Grandpa Coetzee, "but there is Lion's Head standing guard, as well."

Ava noticed that her grandpa and grandma exchanged winks. She tried to guess their secret thoughts, but how could she know? Tucking their smiles away in her memory, she snapped some pictures and stared silently at the vast expanse of Atlantic Ocean. *Dad seems to hate religion. Mom seems a little soft toward it. But only sometimes. Grandma and Grandma Coetzee haven't been near enough to talk about it—until now. How can believing in God change someone's life anyway? What difference does it make? Everyone is going to die somehow. In a car crash, from a disease, at the hands of people who are supposed to love them, as a baby.*

She knew in her heart that the strain between her mom and Grandma Coetzee was definitely caused by religion. What else could it be? This news about Grandpa Amery seemed as vast and important as the majestic view from the top of the towering sentinel, Table Mountain.

Ava always had a way of brightening the mood. "So, Dad, where did you propose to Mom?"

"Let's see, I think I can find the spot fairly easily. I came up here several times by myself scouting out the perfect place. Just follow me," Mr. Zinfield said proudly, tousling Ava's hair and leading the way back up the trail toward a little balcony area that jutted out over the side of the mountain ever so slightly, offering a view of the city below and a thousand miles of ocean.

"We're so glad you are part of our family, Lloyd," Grandma Coetzee said. "Now let's get a picture of the newlyweds. There's no time like the present to make up for lost time."

What does she mean by lost time? Ava noticed the playful elbow jab that her dad gave her mom.

Mrs. Zinfield pulled a picture from her purse from her engagement day over twenty years before. She held it out for Ava to see.

"This is so cool, Mom! You guys have to pose exactly like you did in this picture." Ava took extra care to make sure the poses were the same. "Tilt your head a little to the right, Mom. There. Perfect."

Picture taken, the group headed for the gift shop. *Lost time,* Ava thought. *Why did Grandma say that? Why had time been lost?* She thought about Michael. She'd lost a whole month not speaking to him because she'd listened to Miranda. Picking out a postcard for him, she was still thinking about lost time. *Which one?* The one with the clouds spilling over the top of Table Mountain would be perfect. *What should I write?*

CHAPTER 5

The next day, Grandma and Grandpa Coetzee fulfilled their promise of a trip to the Cape of Good Hope and Boulder's Beach. Ava couldn't fathom what could possibly be greater than yesterday's trip to Table Mountain. Her top ten list would be easy to fill.

"So, are there really penguins in Africa?" Ava asked Grandpa Coetzee as they ascended the trail leading to the Cape of Good Hope.

"There sure are, Ava. And we'll see them this afternoon on our way home from the Cape. But that will be nothing compared to *this* stop." Grandpa Coetzee gently took Grandma's hand as they gravitated toward the lookout points on the cliffs overlooking the "southernmost tip" of Africa.

Now that she thought about it, standing at the end of the world should rank close to number one on her list of top ten. But Ava already knew that *this* stop wasn't the *southernmost* tip. The *southernmost* tip was 155 kilometers southeast at Cape Agulhas. But never mind that, because this is where all the tourists came. On the drive to the Cape, Grandpa Coetzee had already told her the history of the Cape of Good Hope, about how Bartolomeu Dias had been on a mission from the Portuguese to find a route to India around the Cape of Africa. Dias had landed at this cape in May of 1488 on his way back to Portugal. He never actually made it to India, but he concluded that all one had to do was keep going north after rounding the tip of Africa. As it was, Dias' ships were nearly destroyed on the rocky cliffs of the cape, and so he named the place he landed "Cape of Storms."

King Juan of Portugal thought "Cape of Storms" was a terrible name, because who would dare to pass through such an infamously-named place to discover a route to India? The name alone would fill any sailor with fear. So King Juan changed the name to Cape of Good Hope.

Reverse psychology. Ava liked King Juan already. Just as she did, he leaned toward the bright side. But then again, wasn't King Juan leading people to believe a lie? After all, it *was* a stormy cape to pass through. But why not give people hope?

Grandpa Coetzee continued his narrative. "Vasco de Gama, July 1497. This was the next brave adventurer and sailor who dared to sail the entire route from Europe to India."

Ava's ears had perked up at the sound of the familiar name. Ava couldn't remember anything else she'd learned about Vasco de Gama. She'd have to find out more about this brave sailor who set out believing that he'd reach a destination to which he'd never been. In her journal, she scribbled a note: "Info about Vasco de Gama!"

The group of five stopped to catch their breaths at an intriguing signpost at the top of the cliff. Pointing in all directions, markers indicated the distance to major cities all over the world.

"Check this out! New York is 12,541 kilometers away," Ava exclaimed. Turning southward, she saw only the vast stretch of ocean where Grandpa had said the Atlantic and Pacific waters met. Her family ambled to the edge of the cliff, the edge of the world, and stood, gazing out at the two oceans meeting at the tip of Africa. If she could see far enough, the next thing she would see would be Antarctica. Ava squinted her eyes, trying to imagine she could, indeed.

Ava thought her parents and grandparents were like those two oceans, different and yet the same, meeting somewhere in the middle. She found herself gazing down, down, down the rocky, majestic cliffs into the bright aqua water swirling and crashing on the sand and rocks below. *So beautiful. Is there or is there not a God who created all of this? Michael thinks so. Or is this beauty just a result of the natural processes of evolution? My family sure thinks so. There's no scientific evidence God. People believe what they are taught as children. True enough. There's no harm believing either way, as long as you don't force your belief on people or hurt someone else in the name of your religion. I wonder what Grandma and Grandpa Coetzee believe. She did say that she met Grandpa Amery at a religious meeting. Yeah, but lots of people try religion at some point in their lives. No need to complicate things with religion.*

"Ava!" A loud chorus called her name, and Ava realized that she'd been lost in thought, oblivious to what was going on around her as she considered the meeting of the two oceans, the beauty, her two families. "Happy Birthday!"

Ava turned to face her family. The sound of the wind and surf had allowed them to carry out their plan undetected. Grandma held up an opened jewelry box and Mom snapped pictures of Ava's reaction—wide eyes and a look of confusion and joy.

Taking a step forward, Ava saw one shimmering pearl at the end of a silver chain. The pearl was mounted in a silver circle accented by six tiny diamonds.

"Your Grandpa Amery, Ava..." began Grandma Coetzee. "He owned a jewelry shop. And like your mom told you, he did die fighting apartheid. He was so young. And your mom was only seven."

Ava considered her mom in a new light as her mom steadied the camera to snap another picture.

"It was the most difficult time of my life, losing him. I loved him so much. As a jeweler, he absolutely loved pearls. Not long before he died, he found this pearl on a dive. Diving was a hobby of his. He found only two before this one. He gave that first one to me, and the second, he set aside for your mom when she got old enough. And when he found the third, he said, 'This one is for my first grand-daughter.' What better occasion than your eighteenth birthday while you're here in South Africa?" Grandma ended her speech by taking the necklace out of the case and holding it up against the sky of the Cape of Good Hope.

"It's beautiful!" Ava said, pulling her hair up so that Grandma could fasten it around her neck.

"Happy Birthday, Ava," said Grandpa Cotzee. "I sure am proud to have you as my granddaughter."

"Thanks, Grandpa." Ava couldn't think of anything else to say. She barely knew him. Why had her family not been back to South Africa all these years? It seemed so unfair now. And what an amazing gift—this pearl that her Grandpa Amery had discovered with his own hands.

For a few seconds, no one spoke. Ava could feel a lump forming in her throat. So many unanswered questions and so much joy all in one moment. There was a question burning in her mind, but she couldn't bring herself to ask it. It would be too awkward, especially with Mom and Dad standing right there.

"I didn't think you'd be speechless," Grandma Coetzee chuckled.

"Oh, I am speechless! This is so incredible! Thank you so much." Ava said. "Who says pearls are old-fashioned? This one is absolutely stunning. Wait a second. You said there were two more pearls? Where are they?"

"We thought you'd never ask," Grandma laughed again, reaching for a necklace hidden by her blouse.

"And here's mine," her mom chimed in with girlish excitement. Ava had noticed her mom's necklace when they'd set out earlier that morning. She'd never seen her mom wear it, and she didn't question her when she told her it was a jewelry store bargain.

"You guys planned this!" Ava was laughing and crying at the same time. "Oh my goodness! We've got to take a picture. Dad?" Ava motioned for the camera and handed it to him.

Three generations posed for a picture on the cliffs of the Cape, smiling into the sun, eyes dancing with the water crashing below. Each woman held her pearl out for the camera to capture. Each face radiated joy.

After the photo shoot, Grandpa Coetzee spoke up. "Ladies, I don't want to rush you, but we've got one or two more marvelous stops to make before this day is through. Next stop, Boulder's Beach."

"Don't be in such a hurry, Sweets. Let's enjoy the Cape. I brought a few little treats," Grandma announced.

From her unassuming bag, Grandma produced dried cranberries, nuts, apples, cheese sticks and juice pouches. Everyone was grateful she'd planned ahead. With time to wander and explore, Ava let the beauty of the day soak right in.

A good hour later, Ava and her family, refreshed and satisfied, descended the cliffs of the Cape of Good Hope and headed for the car. Ava reached for her pearl necklace. It seemed just perfect. She couldn't believe Grandpa Amery had actually found this pearl. She'd never owned any pearls before. She'd read in a fashion magazine that they were a little old-fashioned. But this pearl—this pearl was a link to the past, a link she desperately needed. The Cape of Storms had truly become the Cape of Good Hope.

* * *

Ava and her family headed north to Boulder's Beach after the spectacular visit to the Cape. They arrived around three in the afternoon, and Ava was already wondering where she could get another postcard. Every time she saw them, she thought of Michael. Sending postcards would be her way of making up for lost time. The least she could do was help him build his collection.

"Oh my, there really *are* penguins in Africa!" Ava remarked, snapping a picture of a "kissing" pair. Her mom and dad strolled arm in arm ahead of her, pointing out the cute antics of the penguins and no doubt reminiscing about the times they'd been here before, ambling along the wooden boardwalk which led them through the sand dunes and thick vegetation leading up to Boulders Beach, a convenient stop on the way home from Cape Point to Cape Town.

"Ava, come here and I'll give you some facts to go along with your pictures," her grandpa said. "Did you know that all these three thousand plus penguins grew from just two pairs placed here in 1982?"

"That's pretty cool, Grandpa." Ava snapped a picture of a few penguins preening in the sun, their black and white coats making them look very distinguished.

"And," Grandpa added, "the reason they were able to survive is that the fishing companies cut down on the pelagic trawling out in the bay, leaving more anchovies, and that's a big part of the penguins' diet, and…"

Ava was listening as best she could. Grandpa Coetzee seemed to know so many facts, and it was hard to remember them all and keep up with all he wanted to share. *Pelagic trawling?* What was that? Should she ask and risk a *very* long answer? Ava thought of a little innocent idea. "Grandpa, can you explain pelagic trawling in ten words?"

Grandpa Coetzee walked along, brows wrinkled deep in thought. After a full minute, he said, "Catching midwater fish with huge nets dragged behind a boat."

Ava rehearsed the definition in her head and counted on her fingers. Exactly ten words. "Grandpa, you're an expert!" She laughed and surveyed the penguins waddling along the white sandy beach between the huge, granite boulders, smooth and gray in the afternoon sunlight. This was the best time to be here, Grandpa had said, because the penguins were returning from feeding in the bay. Ava appreciated Grandpa Coetzee's extensive knowledge, which always seemed to have them in the right place at the right time.

On the beach area, Ava slipped off her sandals and walked toward a group of penguins perched on a boulder. Just up ahead of her, a group of five or six teenagers posed for a picture with several willing penguins. Ava could see five of the teens smiling into the sun, while a sixth girl with long blonde hair laughed and counted to three for the second time, her back to Ava. *Is she wearing a D.C. shirt? She sure is.* Ava didn't think twice. She walked right over to get a closer look.

"Want me to take your picture so you can all be in it?" Ava asked.

The girl with the long blonde hair turned toward her, camera still poised. "Oh, sure! Thanks!"

"Hey, are you guys from D.C.?" Ava asked hopefully.

"I am, but they're not," the blonde girl said.

Almost like a chorus, the others chimed in. "I'm from Holland," one girl said.

"Texas," the tall boy added.

"Korea," said the boy with rich black hair.

"New Zealand," said a girl with a heavy accent.

"France," said the shortest girl.

"And I'm from... Mercy Ships?" the last girl said.

The others in the group laughed at the last girl's comment.

"Oh, my goodness! Ava's eyes grew wide and she stepped back a few feet to inspect the group again. "So how do you all know each other?"

"We all live on a hospital ship, and we go to school together," the blonde-haired girl answered, still smiling. "I know it sounds crazy, but it's true. And by the way, my name is Jessie." Jessie stuck out her hand.

"I'm Ava. And I'm also from D.C.! I saw your T-shirt and hoped it might be true." Unconsciously, she reached for the pearl dangling from her new silver necklace and dug her toes into the sand, tilting her head into the sunlight, laughing in disbelief. "I'm just visiting my grandparents here in South Africa for Christmas."

"Wow! That's so cool! Really? Where do you live in D.C.?" asked Jessie.

"Forest Hill. Do you know where that is?"

"I think so. I used to live in Capitol Hill, until we joined Mercy Ships. Have you ever heard of Mercy Ships?" Jessie asked.

"No, no I haven't," said Ava. "You'll have to tell me more. Where is the ship now?" Ava scanned the beach.

"It's docked in Cape Town at the V & A Waterfront," the tall boy said. "We're just on a field trip today, but we'll be back on the ship this evening."

"Cape Town is where my grandparents live," Ava said, incredulously.

"You should *definitely* come visit the ship then," Jessie said. "You can't miss it. It's docked in the port in Jetty #2, and we're giving tours of the ship for one more day. Then we'll be headed to Liberia."

"Liberia?" Ava's tone reflected her intrigue.

"Yes, and we'll be there for about seven months," said Jessie. Before Ava could ask, Jessie continued, "Our parents work on the ship, and we go to school onboard. My mom's a nurse, and my dad's a teacher in the academy. He's here at the beach... somewhere." Jessie scanned the beach. "Where *is* he?"

"My dad works in the galley," said the tall boy from Korea. "And let me introduce myself. My name's Shin. Nice to meet you, Ava."

"Nice to meet you, Shin," Ava said, thrilled that she had met such a diverse group of teenagers on a beach in South Africa. This would definitely make the top ten list.

Ava caught sight of her family, who had also taken off their sandals and were strolling along the beach, and waved. They waved back, not perturbed in the least that Ava had struck up a conversation with complete strangers.

"So how will I be able to find you if I come visit the ship?" Ava addressed her question to Jessie.

"I'll write you down as a guest," said Jessie. "And when you get to the check-in, just tell the security worker. They'll check your ID and then page me. Wherever I am, I'll come and meet you in the reception area."

"This is *too* cool," Ava said. "I am *sooo* going to visit this….Mercy Ship."

"Hello, I'm Elise," said the girl from Holland.

"Jacob," said the tall, blonde-haired boy from Texas.

"Sophie," said the girl from New Zealand.

"Lorraine," the French girl said.

"Carissa," said the last girl.

Ava addressed Carissa. "And you said you were from…the ship? What do you mean?"

"I was born in Seattle, but I've lived my whole life on the ship. My dad is the chief surgeon," said Carissa.

"I bet my dad would *love* to come on the tour with me. He's an eye surgeon," Ava told the group.

Jessie's eyes lit up. "Not a coincidence. Yes, bring him. We have eye surgeons on the ship, and I'm sure he'd love the tour, too," said Jessie.

"Yeah, I wonder if *he's* ever heard of Mercy Ships. I'll ask him."

"Ok, we'll be expecting you. In fact, if you come, I'll give you your own personal tour," said Jessie.

"You will?" Ava asked.

"You bet! We're both from D.C. I'll show you the whole ship. Oh, hey, we gotta go—I see my dad waving to us."

"Ok, expect me tomorrow. I'll talk my parents into it, no problem. I'll see you tomorrow. Wait, let me get your e-mail just in case!"

CHAPTER 6

"You and Dad go ahead. The last thing I want... just go... I'm not going." Ava recalled her mom's forced words, spoken with pressure, like the water trapped in a lock, waiting to get out. That was yesterday evening after they'd researched Mercy Ships on the Internet to find out more information. The most intriguing piece of information they discovered: Mercy Ships was a *Christian* hospital ship.

This new day, Christmas Eve, Ava was standing in the long line for an opportunity to tour the Mercy Ship—with her dad.

The gray clouds overhead threatened rain, and old Van Hunks and the Devil were having their smoking contest. If Mom was the water pent up in the locks, Dad was the water crashing on the beach, free and unaffected. Ava was sure his eagerness to come with her was connected to the eye surgeries performed on board. Anytime Dad had a chance to expand his professional expertise, he took it.

Why does Mom seem to want nothing to do with anything religious? Why is Dad even willing to go? He's always talking about how ridiculous it is to believe in a god when science explains things just fine. God is ok for others, just not for him, I guess.

Ava and her dad had been waiting patiently in the long line of people for their turn to tour the ship. The line stretched the length of a football field, Ava thought, but it moved quickly. Finally, they neared the front, and a group of about fifty was escorted into a building on the dock to begin the tour. The loud speakers came to life with a song. Thunder boomed.

A young lady began to tell about the mission of the ship, to bring hope and healing to the poor of West Africa. Ava listened attentively. When the tour guide mentioned God and following the example of Jesus, Ava jabbed her dad's side, and he winked back. *He thinks they're all crazy.*

Ava began to worry that she'd never find Jessie in such a mass of people. She hadn't even e-mailed her.

At the security booth, they gave their names and asked about Jessie. The security officer, looking exhausted from a busy morning, perked up with a smile. He radioed someone and then spoke to Ava and her dad in his thick Asian accent. "Go up the gangway. She can meet you in reception in a few minutes."

The clouds had loosened their hold on the rain, and it fell in large, random drops. Up the long, sturdy gangway, they followed the other tourists, dodging the raindrops.

Ava had never before walked into the mouth of a ship like this. An exquisite cruise ship en route to the Bahamas, yes. But this ship, although humble, emanated a spirit born of beating the odds. "This is so cool, Dad! Just think, you could be a surgeon on a ship like this and we could travel the world."

"Wait right here," a kind woman said in a southern accent. "Ya'll are gonna *love* this tour. Jessie is such a sweet girl. She'll be here real soon to show you the ship."

The rest of the tour group went on ahead, crowded together, wiping off the droplets of rain they'd rushed through to get from the temporary tour building to the gangway. At last they were inside.

Immediately, a glass display captured Ava's attention in the reception area where the nice southern lady had asked her and her dad to wait. First, she noticed the picture of a baby, its upper lip missing and deformed. *Cleft lip.* Ava knew this condition. She'd seen pictures like this before.

In another picture, a woman smiled a radiant smile, like the joy of a thousand people. Ava read the caption above the pictures and artifacts artfully displayed behind the glass: *Like raindrops on a stormy day they fall, from simple and preventable things.*

Ava wiped the raindrops from her arms as she considered the words. *They fall. The people fall. From simple and preventable things. Why? Why is there such suffering in the world? Why can't everything be perfect right now?*

Staring into the eyes of a young boy who carried a bucket of water on his head, Ava felt as if she were peering into the very heart of Africa. The lump in her throat was back.

"Ava? You're here!" cried a semi-familiar voice. It was Jessie— and a tall, slim man with Jessie's same blonde hair.

"Oh, hi! I told you I'd make it," Ava said with a huge smile. "And I brought my dad. Ava gestured toward her dad who had just finished speaking with a woman at the reception desk. "Dad, this is Jessie from the beach yesterday. Jessie, my dad, Lloyd Zinfield."

"And this is my dad, Mark Sterling."

The two dads stuck their hands out and said simultaneously, "Nice to meet you." Everyone laughed and Ava instantly felt more relaxed. She hadn't realized she'd been digging her nails into her palm.

"I have an idea," said Jessie. "Why don't the dads and daughters split up? That way, your dad can see more of the medical side of things, Ava, and I can show you what life is like on the ship for me. What do you think, Dad? Sound good?"

"Sounds great, Jessie. I'll do my best to give Mr. Zinfield the surgeon's tour. I'll find Carissa's dad first. I might teach biology, but I'm no surgeon."

Ava's pulse quickened. "See ya, Dad. Oh, when should we meet back here?"

"I think an hour would be perfect, if you can stay that long," Jessie suggested.

Mr. Zinfield checked his watch. "Uhm, sure. We'll meet back here at noon."

Jessie led Ava down the corridors of the ship, through the holds, past the galley, down a set of stairs, through a small library, and into the academy. Ava couldn't believe she'd come across such an amazing opportunity. Already in her mind, she was writing her next article for her journalism class about the Mercy Ship she'd discovered docked in South Africa on a trip to see her grandparents over Christmas, and she had her camera ready.

Ava took on the role a professional journalist gathering information for her latest documentary. "So, tell me... what's it like to go to school on a ship?"

"It's different, that's for sure. We only have about 40 students total in all the grades, so classes are small. Younger grades stay with one teacher, but high school students change classes. As you can see, this is almost the entire school." Jessie swept her hand out to introduce Ava to the academy. A main room with ten computer stations led into four smaller classrooms, two on either side. "And just think! This used to be the cocktail lounge when this ship was a passenger-liner on the Mediterranean. Back then it was called the *Victoria*, but it's been renamed the *Anastasis* because it was *resurrected* for service. That's what "anastasis" means in Greek—resurrection." Jessie's narrative had a romantic flair.

"How exotic!" Ava said, matching her tone. She took note of the name. "So what are the school hours?"

"We start at eight. Then we get a twenty minute break at ten o'clock up on aft deck by the snack bar. Then it's back to class until noon, an hour for lunch, and we're out by 3:30."

"A break on aft deck? Now that's cool. I hope that's part of the tour."

Mrs. Landers, the assistant principal, waved hello. She was sitting in her office sketching and shading tropical flowers in pinks, purples, oranges, and yellows. A jazzy piano music spilled out into the common computer room.

"What are you doing in here on our day off, Mrs. Landers?" asked Jessie.

"Just finishing up a Christmas present. Tomorrow's Christmas." Her eyes sparkled.

"I just love Christmas on the ship," Jessie said to Ava. The best part is finding all the little gifts outside your cabin door."

"That sounds fun. Who came up with that idea?" Ava asked. In her mind, she relived a D.C., Zinfield Christmas, complete with a live, flawlessly-decorated fir tree and beautifully wrapped gifts beneath. She contemplated what Christmas would be like this year in South Africa with her grandparents.

"It's a Dutch tradition" said Jessie. "You set a shoe outside your door, and people sneak by during the night and place little gifts there—candies, a piece of fruit, handmade cards, trinkets from travels. It's so much fun. What is your family doing for Christmas this year? Do you have any special traditions?"

Ava stopped twirling her hair. "We're going to have a brai, for sure. Mom says that's the South African word for a good old-fashioned BBQ. I imagine we'll just hang out, play dominoes, and eat and talk. My Aunt Sharon and Uncle Rick and my cousin were supposed to come from England, but something came up, and they can't make it."

"It must be pretty awesome to have family in South Africa," said Jessie.

"Yeah, it's only the second time I've been here though. Mom and Dad get so busy with their jobs. And when we do have vacation, we usually go skiing or hiking—not to South Africa." Ava silently contemplated whether it was her parents' busy lifestyles or perhaps something else that had kept them from South Africa all these years. She was beginning to think it was the "something else."

Jessie led Ava out of the academy and up a set of stairs to the aft deck. Ava followed Jessie's lead and peered into the windows of a small classroom.

"This is the third and fourth grade classroom, and *it* used to be the chapel. Pretty cool, huh?"

Ava gazed into the window of the classroom again. *A chapel. Where people prayed to an invisible god. And why?* Ava envisioned people kneeling and making the sign of the cross. She had always appreciated old houses and buildings and spaces because she loved imagining people long-gone living out their lives there, unaware of anything to come.

"Are you ready to see more of the ship?" Jessie asked.

Ava, lost in thought, drifted back to the present. "Definitely," she answered, following Jessie down the long corridors of the ship while she pointed out everything of interest. At last, they followed a few sets of stairs to A deck, and into a cabin marked A143.

"So how long have you lived on this ship?" Ava asked.

"This will be my third year. But we usually go back home in the summer for several weeks and stay with my grandparents in northern Virginia. They live in the country, and I've really enjoyed spending part of the summer with them the last two years." Jessie pulled her long, blond hair back into a pony tail. "After all, my grandpa has horses. So I get to ride as much as I want."

"I've never even ridden a horse," Ava admitted.

"Maybe this summer when I'm home you could come out. Wouldn't that be neat? I think it's absolutely providential that we're both from D.C. It makes you wonder if we've ever crossed paths, doesn't it?"

The cabin where Jessie lived was like a little apartment, small and cozy very much like a tiny, tiny home. "So what's it like living on a *ship*?" Ava was full of questions and thoughts. Above the tiny sink in the kitchen, she couldn't help but notice a calendar tacked to the wall. She read the caption. *IMAGINE hearing the message of the nature and character of a loving God for the first time in your life.* A single bird soared through the orange-tinted sky that illuminated a sea of gray clouds.

"Need to use the bathroom? I do. Hang on, I'll be right back," said Jessie.

Ava's heart burned to ask Jessie about this God, for surely she knew. *But surely there is no God. What about all the suffering? If there were a god, why would he allow it? And besides, scientists have proven much of the Bible to be inaccurate. There are contradictions. Grandpa has told me that. Christians are just a little misguided. They've made up a god, just like all the other religions of the world, to explain why the sun rises. But then, what happens to me when I die? Nothing, Ava. Nothing. I'm sure Jessie is a Christian. She doesn't seem so crazy.*

Neither does Michael. Ava thought of his blue-green eyes. *Why can't people just be good for goodness' sake?*

Ava closed her eyes and saw again the cliffs at Cape Point. She couldn't get enough of the beautiful, blue crashing waters, the vastness of the ocean, the greatness of it all. The scene was fixed in her mind so vividly.

She opened her eyes and stared for a few more seconds at the lone bird soaring through the sky on the calendar. *Maybe there is a creator. No. Ava, get a grip.*

Jessie returned from the bathroom.

"So what was it like the first year you were here?" Ava asked.

"It was hard to get used to at first. Everything was so new. My parents rented out their condo in D.C. and we packed up most of our things and flew here. We didn't know if it would be for a year, or two, or three…" Jessie stopped talking and followed Ava's eyes to the calendar. "Pretty neat calendar, huh?" She removed the pin and took it down, flipping to another page. In the photo, a little girl smiled shyly at the camera, her upper lip bandaged with three white strips, which held her newly repaired cleft lip together. Her arms cradled two huge stuffed animals her same size on either side. "I got to adopt this little girl while she was here."

"Adopt her?" Ava's eyebrows raised and she waited for Jessie to explain.

Jessie just smiled. "Yes. Any crew member can sign up to adopt a patient. Once you sign up, one of the coordinators matches you with a patient and sticks a note outside your cabin door with the patient's name and surgery information. Then you just go visit the patient in the ward after their surgery—you talk to them, play with them, color with them, whatever you think of to do. I've only adopted kids."

"Did they speak English?"

"Some did. Some didn't. My dad says they speak English in the capital, Monrovia, but there are also many tribal languages. Fortunately, there are translators available, so that's not a problem." Jessie seemed lost in thought. Then, after a few seconds, her eyes lit up. "I wish you could visit the ship in Liberia—when it's in service. Then you could see what it's like for yourself."

Ava tried to picture herself sitting face to face with the brave African girl in the calendar. What would she say? Why not dream?

"Maybe I could! I have spring break in April. I would *so* do it. At least I think I would. Could I?" Sometimes Ava found herself saying things just to see how they would sound coming out of her mouth.

"If you're really serious, I'll ask about it. My grandparents came and stayed a week the first year we were onboard, so I know it's definitely a possibility."

Ava reconsidered her hasty words. What would her parents think if she told them she wanted to give up her spring break to trek across the ocean to spend a week on a hospital ship in West Africa? On one hand, she didn't think they'd be surprised. Ava had always talked about her dream to travel through Europe. But to a Christian ship in Africa? And why was Jessie so eager to invite her, practically a complete stranger, to visit? But then again, Ava had felt an instant connection with Jessie. Had Jessie felt the same?

"I'd love to live a week of your life," Ava told Jessie after she'd thought a moment more. "Sounds like you really love it."

"Oh, I *do* love it! I can still keep in touch with my friends back home through e-mail and—and I've made a lot of new friends here. My mom and dad said we might stay two more years." Jessie flipped the calendar back to December. "I guess the best part is seeing people's lives changed, not just physically..."

Jessie had stopped mid-sentence. Ava tried desperately to finish her thoughts, to figure out what Jessie would have said next. She knew it must have something to do with God.

Bringing hope and healing to the poor. That's what the tour leader had said. *Following the example of Jesus. Loving God. Serving others.* No matter where Ava turned, she seemed to come face to face with this idea of God.

It was like staring into a holographic picture. If you stared long enough, your eyes would suddenly focus and the hidden picture would become clear. But nothing was becoming clear. No picture came into focus, but Ava couldn't and wouldn't turn her face away. She just kept staring into the faces of those little kids deformed by tumors and cleft lips and knew that there was something more she needed to see. Something just had to come into focus soon.

"Lives changed? So tell me more about that." Ava followed Jessie from her cabin down the corridors of the ship, eager to hear more.

CHAPTER 7

"Once," Jessie began, "there was a woman who came to the screening day—she had woman problems. I'm not exactly sure of the whole story, but she was leaking urine and had been shunned by her community. Her husband didn't want anything to do with her, and she was desperate for help."

"What's a screening day?"

"That's the day when people from all over the area come to be screened by doctors and nurses on the ship to see if they can be helped." Jessie had led Ava to the dining room. "Come on, let's get a drink, and I'll finish the story."

Jessie breezed over to the drink station, filled her glass with Sprite, and took a sip. Jessie did the same. Ava couldn't help but think they were already like sisters.

The girls sat down at one of the tables near the portholes. Jessie continued, "When the doctors examined the woman for surgery, they told her there was nothing they could do."

"Nothing at all? Was it that bad?" Ava tried to imagine what kind of troubles this woman would have. "So how did the woman develop this condition? Is it common?"

"Sometimes, in a difficult childbirth, the vaginal wall tears because the baby is pushing for so long against the pelvic bone. The hole is called a fistula. It's preventable in most cases because women can have an emergency C-section. But women in poor countries have their babies at home, and when there's a problem, there's no medical care," Jessie explained. "And most of the time," Jessie paused, "the baby is stillborn."

"That's so sad. What happened to the woman? Did the doctors send her away?"

"They tried. They told her they couldn't help her, but she said she wasn't going to leave. She said, 'If you can't help me, then just kill me, because I don't want to live.'"

"Are you kidding? She said that?" Ava was shocked at the woman's desperation.

"Yeah. I can't imagine it either," Jessie said. "The chaplain tried talking to her as well, but she soon realized that the woman had no intention of leaving the ship. So the chaplain told her, 'Ok, come in this other room over here and we will kill you.'"

"What?" Ava's voice raised in disbelief. "Are you serious? They told her they were going to kill her?"

"Yes. The chaplain and another lady escorted the woman into this room to "kill" her as they said. Of course, they never would have done that. But what they did—they started praying for the woman."

Ava sensed that the conversation was coming to this. What could prayer possibly do when the person praying was praying to the empty sky? Her pulse quickened as Jessie unraveled the story of a woman Ava had never met but was already fascinated with.

"For about two hours they prayed, but the woman just wanted to die. It was like a spirit of oppression. But they kept sharing God's love with her. They told her about Jesus' sacrifice for her sins—about how her life could have hope. But she wouldn't accept it. She kept telling them she wanted to die."

Jessie paused, and Ava speculated about what she might be thinking. She thought, perhaps, that her stoic face gave away her disbelief. But still, something in Ava's heart longed to know the outcome.

"So did praying for the woman help things?" It was the only reasonable thing Ava could think to ask. She studied Jessie's face. Her soft, blue eyes were watery with tears. Her voice almost trembled, and yet she smiled.

"Did prayer *help*?" Jessie repeated her question. "It totally changed her life. The woman finally surrendered. She said the name of Jesus and accepted his love and forgiveness. She began to weep. And from that moment on, she didn't want to die anymore. The chaplain told us this story in one of the crew meetings last year. I don't remember all the details, but that story had a big impact on me. It's just so amazing what God's love can do. That's the change I was talking about. The woman still has her problem, but now she also has hope. She left the ship praising God and returned to her community."

"That's... great." Ava knew she didn't sound convincing. She stared out the window at the line of people still waiting to tour the ship.

It was Jessie who broke the silence. "Have you heard of stories like that before?"

"Hmmmm," Ava began. "I can't say that I have. But I think some people need to believe in the existence of God to get through life, and some don't. Your parents are very selfless for doing this kind of work. It's something I would probably love doing. In fact, I already have an idea that I'll write about the work of Mercy Ships for my next assignment in my journalism class."

It was Ava's turn to pause. She had to try to collect her swirling thoughts. She saw the water crashing against the rocks at Cape Point. The bus zooming by in D.C. with the "Why believe in a god? Just be good for goodness' sake" slogan. She heard her grandpa ranting about religion and all its evils. She recalled the lone bird soaring in a sunset sky and the caption on the calendar in Jessie's cabin. And there was Jessie right in front of her, still listening to whatever she might say.

"Please don't misunderstand me. I totally respect people who are religious. But I just don't think it's for me. My family—like my mom and dad, my grandparents—they don't believe in God either. I just don't see a need to believe in God. Science explains all we need to know. It's like religion is just there to keep us from doing bad things. And there's nothing wrong with that." Ava sipped her Sprite. "I don't know. I usually don't ever talk about this much." She was trying to think of how to express what she felt inside. But she couldn't put it into words. She checked her watch. "Hey, it's time to meet back up with our dads."

"Oh, yeah it is," Jessie said. "We're a few minutes late." She scooted her chair back and grabbed their empty glasses. Ava followed Jessie's lead as they left the dining hall, and their fragile conversation, behind.

"Hey girls! There you are," Jessie's dad squeezed her shoulders and gave his daughter a sideways hug. "So, what do you think, Ava? Are you ready to join our crew?" he asked teasingly.

"Uhm, sure." Ava said. "Sign me up! I'd love to join the crew. Jessie and I are going to keep in touch for sure."

"We exchanged e-mails, took pictures, and toured the ship. And I told Ava she could plan on visiting us at Grandpa's this summer in D.C." Jessie told her dad.

The group walked toward the gangway and stepped out into the grayish afternoon. A steamy mist had settled over the city and it seemed strangely quiet

"Look! A rainbow!" Jessie said, pointing towards the mountains over Cape Town.

"Incredible! It looks like it's shooting right out of Lion's Head," Mr. Sterling added.

Ava snapped a picture as she remembered Grandpa Coetzee's warm tone when he spoke of Lion's Head yesterday. She couldn't wait to show him the picture. The rainbow was a perfect ending to the tour, and it would definitely make it into the top ten.

CHAPTER 8

"So how was the tour?" Ava's mom asked so cordially that Ava was a little perplexed. Did her mom truly care to hear? Last night, she seemed annoyed that Ava had pleaded to go on the tour, and now she wanted to hear all about it. Ava sank into the couch across from her mom in her grandparents' living room and propped her feet on the coffee table. Where should she even begin?

"Mom, it was absolutely incredible." Ava sat up to look her mom in the eyes. "Jessie showed me all around the ship. I saw the galley, the library, the academy, her cabin—she even showed me where she does her laundry. There's a little weight room, a post office, a piano room, and even a lounge with a coffee bar."

Ava stopped to weigh her mother's reaction. "There are about 350 crew members on board from probably forty different countries. But the best part was seeing what the ship is all about. Mom, it's amazing. The doctors on board provide free surgeries to people in West Africa who would otherwise never get help. I saw pictures of people with huge tumors, little kids with cleft lips." Ava reflected about whether this would be a good time to bring up the idea of going to visit for spring break. Her mom still appeared to be waiting for more details.

Ava began setting up a spiral of dominoes, a common denominator in the two homes an ocean apart.

"I'm going to write an article about my tour for the school newspaper," she said, after she'd stacked the fourth domino. "And I'm really hoping I can visit the ship during my spring break when it's in Liberia. I thought about it all the way home and …. what do you think?"

"The article sounds appropriate. The visit—I'm not so sure." Mrs. Zinfield picked up the book she'd been reading and flipped to the marked page. "Anything else you want to share?"

Ava could tell that her mom was already worrying about the safety of her only daughter and only child—and not just her physical safety. She knew it wouldn't be easy to convince her to even *think* about letting her go. But she was eighteen now. Did she really need her parents' permission?

"It's just an idea, Mom. Jessie and I only talked about it. She's going to check to see if it would even be a possibility. Please think about it. I *really, really* want to visit the ship when it's in Liberia... if it's possible. You're always talking about how one day I'll travel and broaden my horizons, well...this is my chance." Ava applied her persuasive charm. "Just think about how this experience could launch my career in journalism."

"We'll see, Ava. It seems you haven't thought this through. There's so much involved. You can't travel there alone, for one thing. I'd worry myself sick."

Ava was relieved to see her dad coming inside from helping Grandpa set up for the Christmas brai. Sighing, she tapped a domino, and the neatly arranged spiral toppled into a heap, along with her hopes of traveling to Liberia.

"What's up? You two look like you just got some bad news." Ava's dad squeezed her knee. "What's up, sweetie?"

"I was just telling Mom how I wanted to visit the ship during my spring break," Ava said.

"I didn't think you were serious about that, Ava. I thought you were just saying that to be polite," her dad said, walking over to her mom and putting his hands on her shoulders for a quick massage. "Need a little stress relief?"

"I already have a passport." Ava seemed to be pleading now. "What more do I need? Just... permission?"

Ava knew it was best to let things be for a while. She'd have to control her impulsiveness to make this idea work. Spring break was four months away. She'd give her parents some time to think it over.

But for now, there was Christmas to celebrate with her family in South Africa.

Almost on cue, Grandpa came in through the back door. He had finished setting up for the brai—mowing the small lawn, weeding the flower beds. The sun peeked through the gray clouds that hugged the sky, spreading golden rays into the gray evening.

The smell of oyster stew wafted through the house. Grandma had been preparing a light meal for Christmas Eve dinner. Ava helped set the table, complete with two long, white candles whose flames echoed the golden glow of the setting sun.

After dinner, Grandma Coetzee brewed a pot of decaf coffee and pulled a photo album from the shelf. "Shall we look at some old photos now?"

"Oh," Mrs. Zinfield began, hesitantly, "that would be a great idea. Ava needs to brush up on her family history."

It seemed the photo album hadn't been opened in years. The plastic sleeves were yellowed and some of the pictures fell from their places. On the first page, there was Ava's mom, a tiny baby in a bassinet.

"Aww. Is that you and Aunt Sharon?" Ava asked, pointing at another picture of two girls in blue and white sailor dresses. "How old were you? Five? Aunt Sharon must be about two then. How cute!"

Then suddenly Ava saw it. It was a picture she'd seen a thousand times. The exact picture sat framed on her mother's nightstand. It was the picture of her Grandpa Amery squinting into the sun and holding an oyster shell and pearl. Ava recalled that Grandpa had found three pearls. Grandma had one, Mom had one, and now she had the last one.

"So which pearl is this?" Ava asked. "Yours, yours, or…mine?"

"That's the last one he found," Grandma said.

Ava reached for the pearl on her necklace. "It's this very one?" Grandma nodded.

"This is amazing! This is the best birthday present I've ever received. What other secrets are you two hiding from me?" Ava interrogated them in her journalist's voice.

"Little by little, Ava. Little by little," Grandma reassured her.

Ava saw the candle dancing in her mom's moist eyes.

The evening passed in reminisces and stories and pictures. By ten o'clock, Ava could barely keep her eyes open. The day had been so full, and all she wanted to do was crawl in bed and sink into a deep, sound sleep. She tried to be polite and suppress a yawn, but it was no use.

"Yes, I know. Time for bed, right?" Grandma Coetzee asked.

"Yeah, I'm so tired. I feel like it's three in the morning. Good night, everyone." Ava slipped into the guest room to get ready for bed.

She considered what Michael would be doing right about now. She thought of some questions she wanted to ask him. *What is it like to be a Christian? Why are you so different from the other guys I know? What's your family like? And what about your mom? Why is it just you and your dad? And tell me the best thing about God, in your opinion, if indeed he exists. And what's the worst thing about him? Wasn't he angry at the whole world?*

That last thought disturbed her. She'd skimmed through "Sinners in the Hands of an Angry God" last year in junior English. *And who would want to believe in a god like that? Case closed.*

Before she knew it, she was sound asleep.

CHAPTER 9

On Christmas Day, Ava awoke earlier than anyone in the house. In the living room, the lights on the small, artificial tree twinkled and glowed. She tiptoed to her Grandpa's recliner and wrapped herself in the soft, fluffy robe her grandma had hung in one of the guest rooms for her. Its color reminded her of the dancing waters at Cape Point. That beautiful aqua water.

Ava began scanning the titles of the books on the bookshelf to her right. *Are there any No. 1 Ladies Detective Agency books?* No, she didn't see any. *But what's this?* There, on the third shelf from the bottom, was a black, leather-bound book marked *Holy Bible*. Its cover was worn. *Now this is intriguing. Grandma and Grandpa Coetzee own a copy of the Holy Bible.* She picked it up and set it on her fluffy, sea-colored robe. There wasn't the least bit of dust on it.

Ava had attempted to read part of the Bible—out of curiosity—when she and Mom had spent the afternoon at the bookstore. She'd started with Genesis and scanned quickly to about chapter ten, but she had found the events recorded there to be implausible. She'd shoved the Bible back onto a shelf when she saw her mom approaching, ready to go.

Science had done a much better job explaining how life had evolved. The big bang. Evolution. Fossil records. Carbon dating. Countless scientific studies. Ava had read several of Grandpa Zinfield's articles explaining the logical arguments against the belief in a supernatural force called God. For one thing, he pointed out, people need "God" less and less the more we learn about the world through science. And another major argument resonated with Ava, as well. If God were real, then why were there so many different religions in the world, all seeing and portraying God in different ways?

In spite of her thoughts, Ava decided to give it one more try. After all, wasn't the Bible a best-seller? Maybe she could learn something that would help her understand Michael and Jessie.

Aren't there different kinds of Christians? Like Lutherans, Catholics, Baptists, Presbyterians?

Ava opened the Bible to a random page. Her eyes fell on the big number 12 at the bottom of the page. John chapter twelve. *Jesus anointed by Mary of Bethany,* she read.

Six days before the Passover, Jesus came to Bethany, where Lazarus lived, whom Jesus had raised from the dead. Here a dinner was given in Jesus' honor. Martha served, while Lazarus was among those reclining at the table with him. Then Mary took about a pint of pure nard, an expensive perfume; she poured it on Jesus' feet and wiped his feet with her hair. And the house was filled with the fragrance of the perfume.

But one of his disciples, Judas Iscariot, who was later to betray him, objected, "Why wasn't this perfume sold and the money given to the poor? It was worth a year's wages." He did not say this because he cared about the poor but because he was a thief; as keeper of the money bag, he used to help himself to what was put into it.

"Leave her alone," Jesus replied. "It was intended that she should save this perfume for the day of my burial. You will always have the poor among you, but you will not always have me."

Meanwhile a large crowd of Jews found out that Jesus was there and came, not only because of him but also to see Lazarus, whom he had raised from the dead. So the chief priests made plans to kill Lazarus as well, for on account of him many of the Jews were going over to Jesus and believing in him.

"Ava?" said a voice in the dark.

Startled, Ava snapped the Bible shut. "Uhm, hey Grandpa."

"Woke up early, huh? I see you found something to read."

"Yeah, I just pulled out this…Bible. I didn't think…"

"You didn't expect to see a Bible in my house, is that right?" Grandpa Coetzee guessed correctly.

"Not really," Ava said. "Mom and Dad want nothing to do with religion. I figured you and Grandma wouldn't either."

"Your mom is most likely just hurting inside. She had to grow up without a daddy."

Ava sat in the stillness.

"So have you been out here reading very long, Ava? What part did you read?" Grandpa Coetzee settled onto the couch and switched on a second lamp. He asked the question as if he were familiar with the entire book.

"Something about a man named Lazarus?"

"Go on," Grandpa encouraged.

"It says Jesus raised him from the dead. Then he came back to Lazarus' house for a supper, and a woman named Mary poured expensive perfume all over his feet. A guy named Judas said it would have been better to sell the perfume and give the money to the poor. But he's not really concerned about the poor. He's a thief, and he wants the money for himself. Hey, isn't Judas the one who was supposed to have betrayed Jesus?"

"Yes, he was the one who betrayed Jesus with a kiss. He spent a lot of time with Jesus, but he missed Jesus' heart," Grandpa Coetzee said. "Mary—she came with a heart totally open and broken and ready to receive."

Ava hesitated a moment and then ventured to ask, "Uhm. Grandpa? You're a Christian, aren't you?"

"Yes. Yes I sure am. But you didn't know that, did you?"

"How would I know? Mom sure never mentioned it. Mom and Dad are very much against any kind of religion. Dad's dad, too. But it just doesn't seem… Nothing seems to add up. Lately, I've just…" Ava found it hard to find the words.

"It's ok, Ava. We've seen so very little of you throughout the years. We sent you a children's Bible when you were about eight. Didn't you get it?"

"A children's Bible? I don't ever remember getting a children's Bible." Ava tried to think what would be different about a children's Bible and the one she held in her hand.

Grandpa Coetzee stood up and headed toward the kitchen. "Maybe it got lost in the mail, Ava. I suppose that could have happened. I never asked your mom whether you got it or not, so that's sure a possibility."

The dark hours of morning began to come alive as Ava heard coffee brewing. She didn't know whether she should relieve the ache in her throat and run to the guest room to cry—or just stay there with Grandpa. It was Christmas morning.

Grandpa returned in his soft way to the couch. He picked up the newspaper, folded it unnecessarily, and tapped it on his knee. "It probably got lost in the mail."

"How can a person believe in God?" Ava asked.

"Faith is a gift, Ava."

"So not everybody gets the gift?" Ava asked. "That wouldn't be fair."

"It's not like that, Ava. God invites everyone to believe. He waits for us to open the door. And he stands and knocks. Gently. The Bible says that Jesus is the mediator between God and man. He's how we can be connected to God. Mary—she understood that somehow. She saw Jesus for who He was, the Son of God, who accepted her unconditionally and forgave her sins. She poured out everything she had to honor him."

"I think maybe faith in God is just some peoples' way of getting through life. You know? It hasn't been anything I've needed so far."

Grandpa Coetzee just smiled. "God pursues each of us in a very unique way, Ava. And like I said, faith is a gift. All you have to do is receive it."

"I don't know, Grandpa. The idea seems so strange."

Dishes rattled in the kitchen.

"Sounds like Grandma's up." Grandpa got up from the couch, peered around the corner, and motioned to her. Within a few minutes, Grandma had joined them in the living room with a steaming cup of coffee.

"Why, look what we have here. You two up so early and talking away? Can I join the conversation?"

"We're just talking about... God," Ava said, feeling awkward, noticing her grandma's eyes on the Bible in her lap.

"Ah, I see." Grandma sipped of her coffee. "I suppose it's time I told you a little more about my past. Maybe it will help you understand things a bit more. Especially about your mom and dad. Your mom didn't like it when I mentioned that I had met your Grandpa Amery at church. Did you notice that?"

"Yes," Ava admitted, pulling her robe tighter.

"When your Grandpa Amery died, I died, too, in a way. I couldn't even think straight to take care of your mom and Aunt Sharon. I was so depressed. I even cursed God in front of them. And I sent them to live with my sister for a few weeks while I tried to get through the days. I didn't know how to go on. When your mom and Aunt Sharon came back home, I was a different person. I stopped going to church. I lost my faith. I blamed God for everything. For the accident. For not taking care of my husband."

Ava listened intently as her family's secrets seeped through the dam. Were her mom and dad still asleep? Were they listening in? What if they woke up and heard them talking?

"I spent several years in bitterness. A few people from our church tried to reach out to me, but I shut them out," Grandma confided. "Your grandpa and I *did* meet at church, but we were both visitors that day. After church, all the visitors were invited to a reception with coffee and sweets at the back of the church. It was love at first sight," Grandma chuckled. "We ended up leaving church that day and having lunch together. We laughed and laughed about the fact that we met at church and never went back. We'd found each other, so it didn't seem as though we needed anything else. But after seven years of marriage, we still felt like something was missing, even though we had two children. That's when we went back to church. Your mom was six at the time."

"Was there anything different about church the second time?"

"I think what was different was us, not the church." Grandma Coetzee glanced over at Grandpa. "We were ready to receive. We spent a year in the church, learning and growing in our new faith. And then tragedy came. And I pushed God away. For nearly ten years, I turned my back on God."

"So how did you come back to God after all those years?"

Grandma Coetzee didn't answer right away. She sipped her coffee, and a broad smile spread across her face. "Then they cried to the LORD in their trouble, and he saved them from their distress. He brought them out of darkness, the utter darkness, and broke away their chains. Let them give thanks to the LORD for his unfailing love and his wonderful deeds for mankind."

"I'm guessing that's from the Bible?"

"Psalm 107. Wonderful Psalm. God is so faithful, Ava. I was very distraught when your grandpa was gone, and I wanted nothing to do with God. I was hurt and angry. But God didn't give up on me. One day, when I was home alone—your mom had already left for the States and Aunt Sharon was at school—I was crying out to God. Even after ten years, the pain seemed so fresh. That day, I cried to God, "God, if you are still there, if you love me, if you see me, do *something*. I need you so much." Grandma Coetzee paused. "And then there was a knock at the door—within just a minute. I was so startled. But I walked to the door, and there was a woman from a book club I'd been attending. She said, 'Linda, God sent me over here today to take you to lunch. I hope you'll accept.' From the tears on my face, she knew I was ready. That wasn't the first time she'd tried to reach out to me."

"Wow." Ava didn't have any words to engage her grandmother in continuing the conversation.

"It was just God hearing my prayer, seeing me, knowing my pain, and loving me. I've always prayed God would do the same for you, Ava."

Ava was quiet. She speculated whether coincidences like the one Grandma had just described happened all the time. *Was* it coincidence? Or was it proof that God *really did* exist? After all, hadn't it taken God ten years to answer her Grandma's prayers? Or had it only taken a minute?

"Thanks, Grandma, for telling me all of this."

"You're welcome, sweetie. Now why don't you curl up on the couch a little while. When the sun comes up, we'll celebrate Christmas."

Ava didn't need a second invitation. She curled up on the couch and drifted into a restless sleep.

CHAPTER 10

The sun began to peek through the curtains of the Coetzee house. Ava was just starting to wake up again as she snuggled on the couch with a velvety-soft throw. She could hear her mom and grandma whispering in the kitchen.

"I know you might not be interested," Grandma said, "but today is Christmas Day. And today is also Sunday. So your step-dad and I are going to the ten o'clock service at church. We'd be honored if you, Lloyd, and Ava all came. We could be there as a family. And afterward, we can go to Camps Bay and have a picnic on the beach. It'll be lovely."

We might be going to church? Ava's mind was racing. Grandma hadn't mentioned it until just this moment, and they'd been in South Africa for several days.

"You're not giving up, are you," Ava's mom stated emphatically.

"God never left me, Gwen. He never left you. He loves you. And now your daughter has questions…"

"What do you mean? Have you been trying to convert her, too?"

"Gwen, no. It's not like that. She woke up early this morning and…"

"Fine, we'll go," Ava heard her mom relent. "At least I'll go. I'll leave it up to Ava and Lloyd if they'd like to go or not. I won't make them. Just…don't make a big deal out of it."

Ava yawned and pretended to wake up when they came into the living room a few minutes later. "What time is it?" she asked in a sleepy voice.

"Time for you to decide if you'd like to come to church with me and your Grandma and Grandpa," her mom told her.

The door to the backyard patio opened and Ava's dad came in with a cup of coffee. "Nothing better than watching a sunrise. I can't tell you when the last time was that I actually had time to sit down and watch the sun rise. Now what are you ladies scheming in here? You all have that gleam in your eyes."

"Do you want to go to church? That's the question on the table," Ava said.

"Ah, I see." Mr. Zinfield filled his coffee cup again. "Staying here relaxing with a cup of coffee out on the porch sounds like a better plan to me. I may have to pass."

Ava knew her mom and dad hadn't even had time to discuss the matter, and the idea of going to church was becoming more and more intriguing. She figured she could sway the vote.

"Come on, Dad. Let's just go. Besides, Grandma said that we could have a picnic at the…" Ava stopped herself short.

"You were awake a minute ago, weren't you?" Grandma laughed. "Well, that's quite all right. I don't intend to have any secrets around here. What do you say, Lloyd?"

"We're all coming, Grandma. Right, Dad? When's the next time we will all be in South Africa together? When's the next time Christmas will be on a Sunday?" Ava got up from the couch, gave her dad a big hug, and waited for his response.

"Alright, fine," said Mr. Zinfield. "But just be warned that I'll probably hang out in the lobby… or outside to enjoy the nice weather."

"That's fine, Lloyd. We don't mind a bit," Grandma said. "We'll all be ready to leave at 9:30 then. That gives us a few hours more to enjoy Christmas here at home. I'll have a breakfast casserole in the oven and fresh fruit ready in about thirty minutes."

Grandpa tuned the radio to some Christmas music and Grandma insisted that everyone eat breakfast in their pajamas. A frenzy to get ready followed. Ava's family was getting ready to go to church—for the first time.

Cape Town Baptist Church, the sign read. Everyone got out of the car and headed for the main door. Ava's dad, true to his word, stopped in the lobby and pretended to read some literature on a small table.

Ava scooted into the pew to sit beside Grandma. She scrutinized all the other church-goers and wished she could read their thoughts.

Did they all believe? Were there any like her in the whole crowd who felt nervous and a little self-conscious?

"Are there any rules you have to follow here, Grandma?" Ava whispered.

"No, sweetheart. Just be here. That's enough," Grandma whispered back.

The service was starting.

A man came to the pulpit and waved his hands upward. "Stand, please, as we sing."

The people rose to their feet, and Ava read the words displayed on the screen:

Come, now is the time to worship
Come, now is the time to give your heart
Come, just as you are to worship
Come, just as you are before your God
Come

Ava had never heard the song before. What did it mean to give your heart to God? And was that her Grandma singing? Her voice was sure, strong, and convincing.

One day ev'ry tongue will confess You are God
One day ev'ry knee will bow
Still the greatest treasure remains for those,
Who gladly choose You now

Ava scanned the people around her for clues. *How did someone choose God? What was the treasure? Every knee will bow? Every tongue will confess? When? Where was Dad? Even Grandpa's Zinfield's tongue will confess?*

After a few more songs, the preacher came forward to speak. "We've come to celebrate Christ's birth. We've come to celebrate God becoming human to dwell among us. Immanuel. God with us."

It seemed a long thirty minutes that the preacher talked on and on. Why were all these people here? It was such a beautiful day outside. *Like Grandpa says, people have to make up some way to force people to be good. But people should just be good. For goodness' sake!*

Ava kept reading the banner hung behind the preacher. *Go and make disciples of all nations.*

After the service, Grandma introduced Ava and her mom to several of their friends. Things started to feel comfortable again as everyone started to talk about normal, everyday things over coffee cake and tea. *How has your visit to South Africa been? How's your school year going? So what will you do after you graduate?*

Dad appeared and started to mingle a bit. But that didn't last long. "Is everyone ready to go? I'm ready to relax on the beach." It was obvious he was trying to hide his irritation.

The bright blue waters and warm, white sand welcomed Ava. She kicked off her sandals and let her family finish setting up the big umbrella and blankets. Walking along the shore, she thought about Grandpa Amery. How he must have loved the sea. How she wished she could have known him. Her walk turned into a slight jog. Running felt good. She felt free in this wide open space of ocean and sky.

As she made her way back to the bright yellow umbrella her family had set up, Grandpa Coetzee posed a trivia question as he looked up past the town and barren grass to the rocky cliffs, towering above the beach. "Do you know what those mountains are called?"

"No, but I'm sure you do," Ava teased. "What are they called?"

"The Twelve Apostles." Grandpa Coetzee seemed proud to display his knowledge.

"Hmm...why'd they name them that, I wonder?"

"Don't you know who the Twelve Apostles are?"

"Guess not?" Ava sat down beside him and dug her toes into the warm sand. Her mom and dad stretched out on a blanket, munching away on apples and cheese and bread, staring out into the crashing waves and saying as few words as necessary. Not Grandpa Coetzee.

"The Twelve Apostles were the twelve closest followers of Jesus." Grandpa said that one sentence, and decided to stop talking. He took Grandma Coetzee's hand. Life carried on peacefully when no one talked about such things.

For the next few days in South Africa, no one brought up anything more about religion—except Grandma—and only once. In a way, Ava was glad. After all, religion just divided people. It had kept her mom and Grandma at odds with each other her whole life.

Ava's family spent their last full day in South Africa at Kirstenbosch Gardens, and it proved to be just as delightful as Mom and Grandma had said it would be. Ava had wanted to get an up-close look at the giant protea, South Africa's national flower, but it bloomed in fall, winter, and spring—not in the summer. True. It was winter in D.C., but with the hot sun beating down, Ava didn't have to remind herself that it was summer in South Africa.

When they'd returned home from the beautiful gardens, Ava decided the next best thing to seeing a protea in person, would be to do a little research. That's what a good journalist would do. Besides, she could use little facts like this in an article sometime. She pulled out her notebook and searched *protea* on her grandma's computer.

"Every bit of information is valuable," Mr. Davis, her journalism teacher, had always said. "Gather as much information as you can, because you never know what you might use later."

Aha. Protea. Meaning and Symbolism. Ava clicked on the link. She loved looking up the meanings of things. Flowers. People's names. Ever since she had found out the meaning of her own name, names had fascinated her. Different searches brought different results including "breath of life", "waterfall", and "bird." Each meaning was equally appealing and intriguing.

"So what are you learning about that flower?" Grandma inquired, peering over her shoulder.

It says here that it's named after Proteus, a god of the sea, who was able to know all things past, present, and future. It's also a symbol for *change* and *transformation*, mostly because the god Proteus didn't want people nosing around trying to gain insights from him, so he would change his shape to disguise himself." Ava twirled her hair.

"All those gods and goddesses," Grandma said, with a hint of indignation. The true and living God *does* know all things past, present, and future, but He *wants* us to gain insights from him, and He gave his very life for us." Grandma replied. "The enemy is always trying to counterfeit the truth and lead people astray."

Ava took in her grandma's words, but she didn't respond. How could she argue with someone who sincerely believed that God was real? And that He had an enemy.

"Diversity and courage. In flower language, that's what the protea symbolizes," Ava added.

"Very fascinating." Grandma smiled. "I think I'll take some notes of my own."

Ava studied her grandmother as she wrote. She seemed so peaceful, so confident, so sure.

Ava scribbled her own notes. *Transformation, change, diversity, courage. Proteus, "able to know all things, past, present, and future."*

She didn't know if she was so sure. Or so confident. Or so peaceful.

CHAPTER 11

Ava found it difficult to adjust to the shivery winter of D.C. after the warm, summery week and a half in South Africa, but opening an e-mail from Jessie immediately brought back memories penguins, sand, and rainbows.

E-mail: January 7, 2006

Hi Ava!

I hope the rest of your trip in South Africa was as amazing at the first part. I still can't believe we met each other in the middle of a bunch of penguins on Boulder's Beach. I just know there's a reason we met. This may sound cliché, but I sense that you're a kindred spirit.

How was your Christmas in South Africa? I'm sure it's freezing in D.C. I don't miss that part, to be honest. We are now in Liberia! It's only slightly cooler here than it was in South Africa. It's the middle of rainy season here.

So how serious were you about visiting the ship in Liberia? The possibility is not looking good from my side of the world. I guess I was a little too hopeful that my parents would just say yes, but it's just not a good time. They suggested you volunteer and come for more than a week. Thoughts?

This morning, we visited an orphanage called Alfred and Agnes, and I'll be going out every other Saturday with a team. Today, we told a Bible story, played soccer, jumped rope, braided hair, colored, and blew bubbles with forty or fifty kids. My dad says that so many of the children's parents were killed during the civil war here, and they had no where else to go. It's so sad.

Right now the orphanage is trying to raise money for new dorms because the children are crowded into just one small cinder-block building. Everyone on our team is writing home and asking people to get involved. Any little bit will help. You can help, too, if you want. Just let me know.

In other news, the Liberians have elected a new president—a woman! Ellen Johnson Sirleaf will be the first woman president in Africa. I'm living right in the middle of history! She will be sworn in next week, January 16th.

My dad was saying that the war ended largely due to a group of about 3,000 Christian and Muslim women who petitioned the government for peace. The country is on its way to recovery.

My parents were so glad to meet you on the tour at Christmas. Somehow, you already feel like a long-lost sister. I'm glad I wore my D.C. shirt to Boulders Beach that day. Maybe this summer when I'm home in Virginia, we can meet up at my grandparents' home and you can finally ride a horse. Please write soon!

Your friend in Africa,
Jessie

Clicking on the attachment, she recognized Jessie right away, standing in a sea of little faces. *How fun it must be to spend time with all those precious little kids.* Ava downloaded the picture and saved it on the desktop of her computer. Journalism class was almost over. Ava signed out of her e-mail account, glad for the chance to check it before going to lunch.

She longed to be there with Jessie at the orphanage, but there would be no going to Africa. No reporting from the field. No gloating to her friends that she'd traveled abroad. No incredible experience to put on her résumé to make her stand out from the rest. And she was right in the middle of applying for colleges. When would she have another chance as incredible as this one? *There will be plenty,* she encouraged herself.

Ava grabbed her backpack and headed to lunch. And that's when she saw it. On Mr. Davis' door, someone had posted a sign: *Start the New Year Right! Join Christian Student Fellowship. Wednesdays at 7:30. HERE!*

Here? Michael. She couldn't wait to find out if he'd received her postcards from South Africa. So far, she hadn't even *seen* him today, the first day back from the holidays.

Ava shook off her discouragement with a new plan. She knew what she wanted to do. Would it work? Who would support her? If anyone would, Michael would. Maybe she couldn't *go* to Africa over spring break, but she could make a difference for the children at the orphanage.

Michael was already sitting in front of the deli line. Ava didn't even bother getting something to eat. She had a granola bar in her purse, and that would be enough. She had more important things to consider just now. She *had* to see Michael and tell him everything about the break. For today, Miranda would have to do without her.

"Hey, Ava!" Michael's blue eyes seemed to light up when she approached. "Thanks for the postcards."

"You're welcome." Ava almost tripped over the cafeteria chairs as she tried to sit down. An outburst across from the salad bar area startled her and she lost her balance on the step down and fell awkwardly to the table. Had she heard her name above the noise of the Commons?

"Whoa! Watch out. These crazy chairs are out to get you." Michael was sitting alone, almost as if expecting company.

"Ava? You seem a little distracted," Michael told her.

"Oh, I'm fine, just thinking," Ava said. She didn't want to dwell on the possibility that the outburst had anything to do with her. "How was your break?" she said enthusiastically, pushing down the feeling of awkwardness.

"Thinking about what?" Michael asked, turning the attention back to her.

"I have a LOT of questions," Ava said, scooting her chair closer to block out some of the noise. "And there's so much to tell you about my trip to South Africa."

"Ok, then, you first," Michael grinned. He took a bite of his turkey sandwich while Ava recounted the beauty of Table Mountain, the surprise of meeting Jessie from Mercy Ships, and the tour she'd taken onboard. Michael hadn't even had time to respond.

"And you'll never believe this. I just came from my journalism class and when I checked my e-mail, there was a message from Jessie. She wants me to come to visit the ship while it's Liberia, and I really want to go…"

"That's awesome!" Michael chimed in. "Wow, it's incredible what can happen in a few short weeks. I've heard of Mercy Ships."

"But…" Ava added.

"But what? You're going, right?" Michael challenged.

"Her parents said they'd be too busy that week."

"So…" Michael paused, thinking. "Can you *volunteer* to go on your own? What's the minimum age to volunteer? Eighteen? Are you eighteen yet?"

"I just turned eighteen over the break, and… Jessie's parents suggested the same thing."

"Well, then, why don't you apply?" Michael offered.

"Maybe I will." Ava pulled out the granola bar and envisioned herself walking up the gangway of the Mercy Ship. *Apply. Apply. Apply. That should be easy enough. What could it hurt?*

"Ava. Ava? What are you thinking about?" Michael waved his hand in front of her face.

Ava's eyes lit up. "I almost forgot! Jessie is raising money for an orphanage that needs new dorms. And I've decided to help. Do you want to help? I'm going to write an article for the school newspaper, and then I'm going to set up donation boxes in the cafeteria and the office and…" Ava looked around.

"The library?" Michael offered.

"Yes. The library. Perfect idea!"

"I could make the donation boxes for you. I'm fairly *handy* with hands-on projects." He chuckled.

"Seriously? You would do that?" Ava smiled. "Thank you so much. For some reason, this really means a lot to me. So much has happened."

"I'm glad to hear it." Michael paused. "So, what's going on, Ava? When I talked to you before Christmas and mentioned starting a Christian club, you told me you couldn't believe there is a God; but now you're all excited about this Christian ship. Please tell me more."

"You see, it's all a bit complicated," Ava told him. "I just want to help the kids who've lost their parents in the war. And I think what Mercy Ships does is incredible. That's why I'm excited. The complicated part is that I had no idea anyone in my family was religious. And then, over break, I found out that my mom's parents are Christians." Ava didn't know how much more to share, or what to share for that matter.

"Why don't you come to our group on Wednesday mornings. We meet in Mr. Davis' room at 7:30." Michael handed her an aqua-colored flyer announcing the new club.

"Yeah, I saw the poster on the way to lunch. Maybe I will." Ava shifted uncomfortably as Michael's eyes met hers. "Hey, why don't you come meet some of my friends from the *Beacon?*" Inviting Michael to her usual lunch table seemed the easiest way to get out of asking those questions she'd told Michael she had.

"Ok, lead the way," Michael answered with that winning smile.

Ava had second thoughts about her spontaneous idea, but it was already too late. Michael had those aqua flyers in his hand. Fortunately, there were only about five minutes left for lunch. When she and Michael approached the table, her friends were laughing hysterically about who knows what.

"Hey, everyone," Ava interrupted. "This is Michael. You might have seen him around."

The group welcomed Michael and the laughter faded.

In his hand, Michael held the aqua flyers.

"Whatcha got there?" asked Jeremy, ever the curious one of the group.

"Ah, just some flyers. I got permission to start a Christian club before school. First meeting is tomorrow. You interested? Here's your official invitation." Michael handed Jeremy one of the flyers.

"Church just isn't for me, man. I went once and I swear I'm never going back. That stuff kind of freaks me out. No offense," Jeremy answered.

Another of Ava's friends raised his hands and slowly backed away. "I'm out. Anyway, I have chess club then."

"What is the whole Jesus thing anyway?" Janessa asked. "All we do on Christmas Day is throw presents at one another and get in arguments."

"Jesus was a good man," Travis added. "But I'm not sure he's relevant for today."

"That's not true," Julia piped in. "I use meditation to help me calm down and relax in my crazy family. I'm very open to spiritual things. People need spiritual things."

Ava had never known the extent of all of her friends' beliefs. She turned to Michael.

Michael didn't seem phased. He just asked again, "Okay, who would be interested in having some spiritual conversations?"

Everyone was quiet for a moment. Brendan spoke up first. "I'd be interested. I just want to know why God would send people to hell. I used to cry myself to sleep when I was five years old because my family told me I'd go to hell if I didn't accept Jesus." Everyone laughed uncomfortably—even Brendan.

"Fair enough," Michael answered.

Ava expected Michael to say more. To defend God. To make a case. But he didn't.

"You're all welcome to come to the meeting Wednesday morning. We'll talk about it."

"Oh, look at the time. I think I gotta go work on my history project," Jeremy announced.

Miranda had been quiet up to this point. It wasn't typical lunch-table conversation. She glared at Ava and then averted her eyes. The bell rang, and Miranda gripped Ava's elbow and pressed into her as they headed toward 5th period English. "*What* are you *thinking?*" Miranda asked, once they were away from the lunch crowd. "Are you going religious on me? What about our plans to have fun when we're young? We're about to go to college, remember? If you get involved in all that religious stuff, you'll miss out on all the fun. And for what? Nothing! Trust me, my cousin told me so."

"I don't know, Miranda. A lot has happened over the break. And hey, sorry I didn't eat lunch with you today. I just had to see if Michael got my postcards, and then we ended up talking. And who said I was being religious? I was just having a conversation."

"Yeah, I *saw* you over there talking to him. We've been friends a lot longer than you've known him, and *he's* the first one you want to talk to at lunch? I just figured I was giving you space to flirt with a guy. After Torin, I was just glad you were talking to *someone*. But I'm not so sure he's the kind of guy you want to date." Miranda chattered on. "Seriously, you want a *nice* guy, but not some religious guy. You'll never have any fun."

"Who said anything about dating? I barely know him. And anyway..."

"What?" Miranda probed.

"Nothing. Just....don't you believe that there might really be a God?" Ava asked.

"Ava, you have *got* to stop all this talk. Look at me and tell me you don't believe in some make-believe god," Miranda said.

"I don't," Ava said.

"You don't what?"

Ava stumbled on her words. "I don't....believe in a make-believe god."

"Thank goodness!" Miranda answered. "Now we're getting somewhere!"

CHAPTER 12

January 12, 2006—Thursday

Dear Jessie,

Thanks for your e-mail! I would love to help collect money for the orphanage. In fact, I'll be writing an article about Mercy Ships for our school newspaper, and when the newspaper comes out, I'm going to set out donation boxes around the school. What do you think?

About spring break—it's ok. I understand. My parents weren't thrilled with the idea either. It's not practical to come for such a short time.

Did I actually tour the ship with you just a few weeks ago? I think you'll appreciate the next thing I'm going to share. You asked about my Christmas in South Africa. On Christmas morning, I found out that my grandparents are Christians. How I never knew this is beyond me. But it's true. I had a long talk with my step-grandpa and my grandma about our family. Now I know why my mom and my grandma weren't always on speaking terms. They were arguing about religion.

But the funny thing is, I've never felt closer to my family than when we all went to church together in Cape Town. I never expected that I, Ava Zinfield, would go to church for the first time in South Africa—with my family.

And I'm not even finished. When I got back to school after the break, this guy named Michael invited me to Christian Student Fellowship, and I went to the first meeting yesterday.

I went because Michael stuck up for me earlier this year, and I didn't want to let him down. I thought there would be a handful of students, but Mr. Davis' room was packed. I slipped in the back and listened as a woman taught us from Mark chapter six. She told about Jesus having compassion on a big crowd of people—because they were like sheep without a shepherd. People brought all their sick to him, and all they had to do was touch the hem of his clothes, and they were healed.

I'll write more later. I have to get to work on this article about Mercy Ships—I'm writing you in my journalism class, but I have permission, don't worry. You're an important part of my research. I'm going to check out the Mercy Ships' website now and get some info from there. Write again soon! —Ava

Ava hit "SEND," signed out of her e-mail, and googled "Mercy Ships." She clicked on the link to the website and immediately images of disfigured children flashed on the screen.

A huge tumor had overtaken a young girl's face and she looked miserable. "*Before. After*," the captions read. In the "after" picture, in place of the hideous tumor, a few beautiful scars and a beaming smile of joy told the story well.

Ava scanned the links on the top of the page. *About Mercy Ships. Give. Volunteer. Pray.*

Her eyes locked in on *Volunteer. Apply. Apply. Apply.* She clicked the link.

It wouldn't hurt to learn what it takes to be a volunteer. She was gathering facts for her article anyway. She clicked another link: *What it's like.*

You will work hard, long hours. You will be pushed to your limits. Your heart will break with compassion for those you are serving. But you will find tremendous fulfillment working closely with colleagues from around the world to make a difference by showing mercy to the world's forgotten poor.[1]

What did it take to apply? Ava mused. She clicked another link, *The Application Process*, and scanned the information. *So you have to raise support? And undergo a medical review, a chaplaincy review, and a department head review? Hmm…I don't know if I'd make the cut. I'm not even a Christian, and it's a Christian hospital ship.*

---

1 Quoted from Mercy Ships' official website.

How to Volunteer. She clicked the link. A short fill-in-the blank form popped up. "Thank you for your interest in serving with Mercy Ships! Fill out the form below and we will get back to you promptly."

That would be simple enough. Ava typed in the information. She was just "interested," not "going." *Name, first and last. E-mail. Country. Profession.*

What was her profession? Ava scrolled through the list. She wasn't a teacher, banker, doctor, nurse, plumber. *Aha. There's what I will be soon.* She selected *Student—College.*

Availability Start Date. Availability End Date.

Maybe I could go this summer. It did say volunteers came anywhere from two weeks to two years or more. I could work in the galley. Ava laughed aloud. She hit *SUBMIT.*

Now she would just wait to see what would happen. Maybe nothing. Maybe she would just get a phone call from someone who could give her more information for her article. But since she'd personally been on a tour, much of her information would come from first-hand knowledge. Ava pulled up a Word document and started typing.

CHAPTER 13

When Ava got home from school that afternoon, she tossed her backpack on the chair next to her desk in her room and curled up on her bed with a soft, fleece blanket. There was always an hour or so before her mom got home in the evening from her administrative job at the hotel. And Dad would be home soon after that. She hadn't slept well the night before, and with a light snow falling, a little nap seemed perfect. Her eyes were so heavy.

"Ava, come this way," said a friendly, young nurse "They're ready for you. Your eyes will be as good as new after this."

Ava wore jeans and a T-shirt. *Surely I'm not the patient,* she thought.

The nurse led her into an operating room. Where was her dad? Instead, Ava saw an unfamiliar doctor prepping some tools.

The nurse helped her onto the operating table and Ava lay back, confused. "I can see just fine. I think this is all a mistake!" she protested. The nurse flipped on a bright light above her. Ava struggled to get up as the nurse placed a breathing mask over her mouth and nose.

Ava couldn't move. She started to panic. Turning her head at the sound of the door being opened, she finally saw a familiar face. "Jessie?"

Jessie came to her side and squeezed her hand. "Hey, Ava. I know you're scared. This is a risky surgery, but I'm going to pray for you. Is that okay?"

Instantly, Ava felt peaceful. She let her body go limp as she closed her eyes. "Sure," she said. "Thank you so much for coming. You came all the way from…"

"Ava! Ava, where are you?" Someone was calling her name. "Are you upstairs? You got a package in the mail!"

Ava awoke with a start. She gasped and glanced at the clock. Mom was home. "Coming!" she hollered, ambling down the stairs to the kitchen.

"Hey, Mom. I was just taking a little nap. I had trouble sleeping last night, and I was so tired after school."

"Oh, I'm sorry. I didn't mean to wake you up. You got a package from Grandma and Grandpa Coetzee. Maybe a late Christmas present?"

Ava picked up the package and shook it gently. She cut through the tape on the edge of the box and slid out the contents. Inside the packing box was another box that had fit snuggly inside. She opened that box and there, in leather turquoise the color of the sea at Cape Point, was a Holy Bible. Her very own Bible. Etched in gold letters in the right-hand, bottom corner was her name—Ava J. Zinfield.

Mrs. Zinfield was quiet at first. Ava opened the front cover and read the inscription: *To Ava, A Pearl of Great Price. From Grandma and Grandpa Coetzee, January 2006.*

Ava reached up and closed her fingers around the pearl dangling from the silver necklace Grandma and Grandpa had given her for her birthday. *How thoughtful of them! To think of me as a costly pearl.* Ava felt even more connected to South Africa now.

"That's a thoughtful gift," Ava's mom said, briefly noting the inscription. Ava couldn't determine whether her mom was genuinely sincere or just being polite.

"We better get dinner started, Ava. Will you make a salad? I'll start some steaks."

"Sure, Mom." Ava retrieved a bag of mixed greens, along with a half of a cucumber, a bell pepper, tomato and some onion. "I started working on an article about Mercy Ships today in Mr. Davis' class."

"That sounds like fun. I'm sure you'll have tons of great details." Mrs. Zinfield turned on the stove to heat the skillet for the steaks.

"I know it's not possible to visit the Mercy Ship during my spring break— But I've been thinking…" Ava sliced into the bell pepper. "If I can't visit the ship, why don't I just volunteer? After all, I'm eighteen. Maybe I could go this summer."

"Oh, Ava. Anywhere else. Not Africa. Not Liberia. Dad and I will send you to Europe and you can visit your Aunt Sharon. She'd love to have you visit since they didn't get to see you at Christmas."

"And so...I just filled out a request for more information, is what I was going to say." Ava began chopping up the tomato.

Mrs. Zinfield was quiet. She placed the steaks on the skillet.

"Mom, I need you to support me. I'm not saying I'm *going*. I'm just saying I was *thinking* about it. It's worth a try, right? I just requested more information. That's all I did. Besides, if someone calls, I can get more information for my article."

Mrs. Zinfield crossed her arms and gazed out the window at the falling snow. Ava could see the light from the bright snow reflecting strongly in her watery eyes. But her eyes also held a certain resolve. "Watch the steaks a few minutes, please, Ava. I'll be right back."

Within a few minutes, Ava's mom returned, a plain white box, worn and faded, in her hands. She held it out to Ava. "This is for you."

Taking the box, Ava puzzled over her mom's unusual behavior. "What is it?" She pulled back the lid and lifted the yellowed tissue paper to reveal a brightly decorated book. "Oh, my goodness. Grandpa told me he sent this years ago. It's the children's Bible!"

"He told you he sent it?"

"Yes, yes he did. Christmas morning, I got up earlier than everyone else, and..." Ava flipped through the pages, recalling grandpa's black leather-bound Bible.

"I'm so sorry, Ava. I should have given it to you because it was a gift from your grandparents. But I just don't believe this stuff anymore. I didn't want you to be bothered with it either." The tears were gone from her eyes.

"It's okay, Mom. I understand. After all, it is a bit ridiculous to believe in a bunch of animals fitting on an ark while the whole entire world was flooded." Ava laughed a little, lightening the mood. She examined the cover of the book. An ark, two alligators, two monkeys, two geese, two cats, two birds. A few cartoonish characters. And a rainbow.

Immediatley, the rainbow she'd seen in South Africa right after she and Dad stepped off the ship from the tour flashed across her mind. There was so much she didn't understand.

"I'll take these to my room." Ava scooped up both Bibles and disappeared up the stairs.

CHAPTER 14

Ava settled into her journalism class and opened her e-mail, excited that Jessie had written her back.

Saturday, January 21, 2006

Hi, Ava! Sorry it's taken me so long to respond. I have no good excuse. Thanks for sharing about all that's been going on in your life. It sounds like God is definitely speaking to you. What do you think? That's amazing to hear about your grandparents being Christians. But I'm sorry about the conflicts it seems to cause in your family. That must be hard. I know in some countries, daughters and sons are disowned if they dare confess that they believe in Jesus.

A few weeks ago, the speaker at our community meeting was talking about the difference between religion and relationship. Religion, he said, is anything we do to make ourselves acceptable to God, but Christ has already made us acceptable, so we don't have to do enough good things to get to God or be accepted. People think of religion, and it's a real turn-off. But if you think of it as a relationship, then it's all different somehow. Does that make sense? I'm still thinking about it all myself.

Hey, thanks for helping collect donations for the orphanage. We went again today and told the kids the story about Zacchaeus, a very wealthy tax collector. One day, when Jesus was in his town, he tried to get close to him. But he was so short that he couldn't see over the crowd. So do you know what he did? He ran ahead of the crowd and climbed up a tree. He knew Jesus was going to be coming that way.

When Jesus passed by the tree, he stopped and told Zacchaeus to come down because he was going to his house to eat dinner. You can probably imagine Zacchaeus' surprise. All the people were complaining because Jesus was going to eat with a sinner. But Zacchaeus was so transformed by the love and acceptance that Jesus had for him that he told Jesus he was giving half of all he had to the poor, and that he was going to repay four times the amount to people he'd stolen from. He gave up his deceptive life for a new way of living.

I guess what I'm saying is this: "Jesus came to seek and save the lost." You can find that in Luke 19:10, right along with the story of Zacchaeus. It's pretty cool that he seeks us. It's all about relationship, really. Zacchaeus was looking and so was Jesus.

I have to go now. It's lunch time here. If you have any questions, just ask. I'll try my best to answer. Write soon. —Jessie

Ava read the e-mail again. Should she tell Jessie about her dream? What did it mean? Dreams were just dreams. People dream to sort through all the events of the day and try to make sense of them, right? Yes, probably so. And Ava knew she was trying to make sense of all the things that had been happening in her life. But she didn't quite know how to respond to Jessie just now.

She needed to proofread her Mercy Ships' article and finalize it for the winter publication of *The Beacon.* Today was her deadline— Monday, January 23rd, Mr. Davis had said.

But wait. There was another e-mail, this one from Mercy Ships. She opened it and quickly scanned the message.

Dear Ava,

Thank you for your interest in serving with Mercy Ships. Attached is an application. Please print it, fill it out, and mail it to our office in Lindale (see address below). We will call you when we receive your application by mail.
Sincerely,
Maria Plum,
Human Resources

Ava closed her e-mail and started proofreading. *Sounds like God is speaking to you.* Jessie's words echoed in her mind. How did Jessie know that? It's not like God was just speaking in plain English. And what did she mean, *it sounds like God is speaking to you?* How does God speak to a person?

"Can I print something, Mr. Davis?" Ava asked her journalism teacher.

"Sure, how many pages?"

"I'm not sure, uhm, let me see. Ten?"

"Go ahead. Is it an application?" Mr. Davis asked. He was always encouraging his students to apply for colleges.

"Yes, it's an application all right," Ava told him.

Ava snatched up the application before anyone could see it and ask questions. She slid it into her folder and put her folder in her backpack. She'd read through it when she got home.

She didn't see any way she could improve on her article about Mercy Ships. It was ready to be published. Two peers had read it and approved it, as well. With the few extra minutes she had left in class, Ava pulled up the Mercy Ships' page again and started clicking on volunteer links. What was this? She hadn't seen *this* in her research.

FAQ: Can I apply if I am not a Christian or currently not attending a church?

Yes? I can? Ava reread the answer: *We regularly have non-Christians and/or those who are not currently a member of a church apply to volunteer. Although the vast majority of our staff and volunteers are followers of Jesus, we will consider all applicants. At the discretion of the Managing Director, non-Christian volunteers may be accepted short-term, based on their skills and our needs.*[2]

What a relief! Ava thought. *I'd hate to have to pretend to be someone I'm not. Maybe I really will fill out the application.*

Ava got home and climbed the stairs two at a time up to her room. She sat down at her desk and pulled out the application. Selecting her favorite pen, she filled in her name. *How hard can this be? I'll just*

---

2 Quoted from Mercy Ships' official website.

fill out the application and send it off. No need to tell anyone. Chances are, Mercy Ships won't accept me. But I'll never know unless I try. And this is the only way I'll be able to get to the ship while Jessie's there. Didn't she say she was coming home for the summer though? I've got to remember to ask her when she's leaving next time I write.

First serious question: *Why do you desire to be a volunteer with Mercy Ships?*

Ava wrote, "I had the privilege of meeting one of your crew members in South Africa (Jessie Sterling) while I was visiting my grandparents there. She invited me on a tour of the ship and I was amazed at the work of Mercy Ships. I am also very interested in a career in journalism and this seems like the perfect opportunity for me to serve people, reconnect with Jessie, and practice my journalism skills."

Second serious question: *Tell about your salvation experience.*

Ava thought this question was a little unfair. After all, she'd read that a person didn't *have* to be a Christian to volunteer. Salvation. What exactly did that mean?

She wrote, "I am currently exploring the Christian faith, but I am not a Christian. I hope this does not disqualify me from volunteering. Your FAQ section on your website said that it wouldn't."

There were numerous other questions about health and behavior. Ava had impeccable behavior. She knew her references would vouch for her. She had no pastor, but Mercy Ships had said that that was okay, as well. She could use a mentor instead. Perfect. Mrs. Natalie, her gymnastics teacher for all of her growing up years, would work just fine.

Works well under stress, check; team player, check; respect for other cultures, check; respect for authority, check; flexibility. Ha! I should get a perfect ten on that trait. Ava amused herself as she read through the reference pages. She'd send those off as soon as she could. What was Mrs. Natalie's address? *I'll just drop it by the gym.*

Within a week, Ava had her application to Mercy Ships and her reference letters sent off. Now all she had to do was wait.

CHAPTER 15

Mid-February brought the dreariest part of winter. Ava was so tired of the snow by then that she longed for the hot days that Jessie spoke about in Liberia. The country was so near the equator that it just had two seasons, Jessie had said. Rainy season and dry season.

If anything, it was "dry" season for Ava's project to fund the orphanage in Liberia. She and Michael had set out three donation boxes on the same day that her article had been published in *The Beacon* nearly two weeks ago. Every day, Ava had checked the handmade boxes, complete with locks, because Michael had given her the keys. She knew she'd been cold toward him since then, only answering "not much" or "not much more" when he asked how the donations were going. But he never pressed her for anything more. She could feel Miranda monitoring her every move, and Ava wanted to prove to her that she wasn't falling for some religious guy. She stuck with her own crowd at lunch and even cut back on e-mailing Jessie. But she wasn't happy.

On a blustery Monday at lunch, Ava marched over to Michael's table and pretended like the vast ocean of silence between them hadn't existed. "Why didn't we think of it before, Michael?"

"Think of what?"

"Think of putting pictures on the donation boxes," said Ava. "If we put pictures of the kids on each box, I think people would be more likely to give. Jessie sent me a picture of the kids last month when she told me about the project. I don't know why I didn't think of it before."

"Good idea! And you know what? You never told me how much you wanted to raise. Do you have dollar amount in mind? We could make a poster showing how close we are to reaching the goal," Michael suggested.

"Is five hundred dollars too much to expect?" Ava asked.

"I have no idea," Michael admitted.

"Oh, I have another great idea, Michael. Let's take group picture of everyone who gives and tell them that we'll send the picture to the kids in Liberia," Ava added, feeling alive. *Breath of Life.* She thought of the meaning of her name. This project was *giving* her life. Maybe that's why she had carried things this far. An article. A campaign. An application. What would be next?

By the end of the day, Ava could barely contain her excitement. As she sat through 7th period government/economics, her mind strayed from the principles of supply and demand. *I wonder what Michael's name means.* Tomorrow, she would find out. And tomorrow was Valentine's Day.

Later that evening, as Ava set the table for dinner, her cell phone rang.

"Hello? Yes, this is Ava. Oh, uhm, hello! Wonderful! That's good to hear! No, I can't talk at the moment. We're about to eat supper. Can I call you back? Okay, perfect. What number should I call?"

Ava jotted the number down on the pad of paper on the bar, tore off the note, and slid it in her pocket.

"Who was that?" her dad asked.

"Ah, that was Michael…from school. He just wanted to tell me that he's got the posters all ready for tomorrow. He said that they look…really amazing."

"We're proud of you, Ava," her dad commented. "We're glad you're raising money for the orphanage. You have a big heart."

The rest of dinner revolved around talk of colleges and which one would be best for Ava. Her mom and dad definitely had advice, and Ava pretended to be interested and engaged in the conversation, but all she could think of was "the call." What would she do now? She couldn't keep it a secret forever.

Dishes washed, kitchen spotless, Ava retreated up to her room. She wasn't ready to call the number she'd jotted down. She'd give it a day. Instead, she pulled out a box from her closet with scrapbook odds and ends. She chose a white card stock paper and folded it in half. Cutting out a pink plaid heart, she smiled.

She added swirls in black on the front in each corner, with the big plaid heart in the middle. On the inside, she added a few smaller hearts in various reds and pinks and sat for a long time thinking of what to write.

Happy Valentine's Day. You're Awesome! No.

Happy Valentine's Day. You're a great friend. Not quite.

Happy Valentine's Day. Thanks for being a great friend. Perfect.

She finished the card and placed it in her journalism notebook. Tomorrow, she'd look up the meaning of Michael's name and write it in the heart on the front of the card.

The next day, Ava glided down the hall to her 4th period journalism class. She'd been looking forward to it all day. As she hoped, Mr. Davis left ten minutes at the end of class for "personal business," as he liked to call it.

The class knew that was code for, "You can check your e-mail if you'd like. Or research colleges. Just don't cause any trouble."

Ava opted for e-mail. She knew she needed to write Jessie back, but Jessie had already written again.

Dear Ava,

Hey girl! I haven't heard from you in a few weeks. I hope you're doing alright. You must be busy. Anyway, what's going on in D.C. these days? Are you having any success raising money for the orphanage? Thanks so much for helping out.

I've been praying for you. And I want to encourage you to seek God. His message is love. His mission is forgiveness. To bind up the brokenhearted. To proclaim liberty to the captives, and to open the prison doors to them that are bound. To those bound in sin, he wants to give freedom. Freedom from Satan's evil grasp and countless lies (see Isaiah 61). He comes as our Savior. He says, "Here I am! I stand at the door and knock. If anyone hears my voice and opens the door, I will come in and eat with that person, and they with me." (Revelation 3:21) That's real relationship.

God will not give up on you. You are precious to Him. If you want to stand with Him on his unshakable foundation, then tell Him so. I know you must have questions. Please ask me! I want to help.

I hope you are doing well. Just checking on you. And Happy Valentine's Day! Looking forward to hearing from you!!
Your friend,
Jessie

Ava sat a minute, soaking in Jessie's words. She hit reply. She hadn't known what to say before.

Hey Jessie,

Thanks for your e-mail. I know I should have written sooner, but I just didn't know what to say. Guess what?? Mercy Ships called me last night because I mailed in an application about two weeks ago, and they want to talk to me about volunteering. Can you believe it? I haven't called them back yet. I didn't even tell my parents that I applied because they don't seem overly excited about the idea. But I have butterflies in my stomach!

About the questions... I'm not sure I know what to ask just now. But I guess if I could ask one question it would be this: How did you become a Christian?

I hope next time I write, I'll have better news to share about donations. So far, we haven't had much response. But Michael and I are going to print the picture you sent and add it to the donation boxes. We're collecting donations until March 1st, and the next day, we're taking a group picture of everyone who contributed. That way, the children at the orphanage can see how many people helped out. If I e-mail you the picture, will you be able to print it out? Do you think people will show up? We'll put a note on the donation boxes telling people to

meet before school in the library so we can take the picture. I'll let you know how it goes. Can't wait to hear from you.
Sincerely,
Ava

Ava hit send and settled back in her chair. Then she remembered. The Valentine. She had planned to look up the meaning of Michael's name and write it on the front. It would only take a minute.

Meaning of Michael, she typed. She hit the first link and scanned the screen. She stared at it in disbelief. Seriously? She felt paralyzed. Her eyes were about to betray her overwhelming emotions inside. The screen started to blur. No. It couldn't be true. Really?

The bell rang. She closed out the screen, slipped on her backpack, and darted out of the room before anyone could ask her questions. A tear streamed down her cheek. Then another. Someone would soon notice. Where would she go to get away?

She pushed open the door to the girl's bathroom, went straight to the last stall, and locked herself in. Pulling down the toilet lid, she sat, her face buried in her hands. In spite of her tears, she smiled. It felt like she'd just received a huge hug she didn't deserve.

Ten minutes passed. Girls and their frivolous conversations came and went. She pulled a mirror from her purse and wiped the black smudges from underneath her eyes. She breathed deeply five times in a row.

Then she pulled the Valentine from her journalism notebook. She'd made sure she had a black marker handy to add the meaning of his name.

With trembling hands, she wrote, "To Michael, Who is Like God."

Ava emerged from the bathroom and headed for Michael's table on the far side of the cafeteria, where he usually sat with Ben, who seemed be smiling more often than not these days. Ava had found herself torn between eating lunch with them and eating lunch with Miranda and some of the *Beacon* team.

"Michael! You'll never guess who called me!" Ava practically ran to him.

"Who?"

"Mercy Ships!"

"Did you call them first or something?" Michael asked.

"No, not exactly. I, uhm....I applied to volunteer with Mercy Ships this summer." Ava slipped the Valentine from her notebook. "I don't know what I was thinking, honestly. I just thought I'd see what would happen, and then they called me last night right before we sat down for dinner, but I told my parents it was you because I was so unprepared, and I didn't want to bring it up to them just yet because I didn't think they'd be very excited about it," she said, all in one breath.

"So what are you going to do?"

"I'm going to... I have no idea! I didn't even call them back! I have something for you, though." She handed him the card. "But I have to go, okay? Not much time left to eat." Ava knew that was an excuse. She didn't have enough emotional energy to stay for Michael's reaction. "Anyway, it's nothing much, but I just had some extra time last night. See you after school? We'll put the pictures on the donation boxes, right? And hang up the posters?"

"Right," Michael said. "I have everything ready. Thank you for the card. I have..."

"Okay! See you then," Ava called over her shoulder. She would skip lunch today.

Ava spent the rest of the day in quiet wonder. In sixth period art, she reflected on Jessie's words. *I think God is definitely speaking to you.* In seventh period government/economics, she thought of the rainbow again. She reached for her necklace and fingered the smooth pearl that Grandpa Amery had found long ago.

The bell rang at the end of the day and Ava headed for the Commons. Michael would be there to meet her and they'd tape the pictures to the boxes along with a note explaining the details for the group picture.

Ava passed the library and almost stopped for a minute to return a book she'd checked out, but she caught a glimpse of Torin talking to a freshman girl by the encyclopedias. She continued to the Commons and leaned against the wall, waiting, gazing up through the windows to the overcast sky with patches of blue.

"Hey, there, Ava. Thanks for the card." Michael seemed to appear out of nowhere. Ava was startled. "That was really sweet. I had something for you, too, if you hadn't run off so fast, but I could tell you'd been crying. What's going on?" Michael walked with her toward the first donation box in the office.

"Ah, it's nothing and everything, I guess. I just didn't know what your name meant until a few minutes before lunch." Ava decided to stop with that.

"Pretty neat, huh? So...what does your name mean?" Michael asked.

"Hmm. Today, I think it means *waterfall*, to be quite honest." She smiled. "I was crying earlier. Get it?" She laughed and reached for a strand of hair to twirl.

"Got it." Michael nodded his head, pulled out a small envelope, and handed it to Ava.

"Okay. Hmmm....what could this be?" Ava opened the envelope and pulled out a gift card. "Java Cup! Yay! Hey, we should go there sometime soon. My treat!"

CHAPTER 16

February 15, 2006

Dear Jessie,

I know, I know. I haven't even given you a chance to e-mail me back. But I wanted to tell you that I called Mercy Ships back last night! They have a position open in the galley, and they said they'd love to have me volunteer this summer. I AM SO EXCITED! I'd have to raise some support, but I could do it. I know I could do it. I just don't think my parents would be very supportive. Not sure what to do, but I'll think of something! What do you think?

And I know this might sound strange, but I had a dream about you last month. I wasn't going to mention it, but somehow it seems significant considering everything that's been happening. In the dream, I was having surgery on my eyes, and you showed up to pray for me. All the way from Africa! What's even crazier is that I could see just fine!

Ava

P.S. I meant to ask you when you are leaving the ship for the summer. I need to know... just in case I find a way to Africa by some miracle! I wouldn't want to miss you!

The day after Valentine's Day, Ava walked with Michael to Java Cup after school. Why hadn't they done this before now?

"Remember, I'm buying!" Ava said sweetly, pulling the gift card from her purse and waving it like a magic wand.

"Of course! I wouldn't stop you," he teased her.

They found a seat in the corner, peppermint mochas in hand.

"I called Mercy Ships back," Ava said.

"What did you tell them?" Michael sprinkled some cinnamon on top of his whipped cream.

"That I'd love to accept the position? It's a lot of money to raise. Close to three thousand." She shivered and warmed her hands on her coffee cup, still shaking off the cold, cheek-biting weather.

"Do you have any money saved up?" Michael asked.

"I have about a thousand in my savings account. It's mostly spending money I earned last summer from working at Ralio's Pizzeria—and birthday money."

"Aww! You worked at the pizzeria? That's cool!"

"Yeah, my parents have money, but they don't just hand it out for anything. They pretty much told me that I had to work for it just like they did," Ava said. "And I still haven't even told my parents that Mercy Ships has tentatively accepted me."

"You haven't told them *anything?*"

"Only that I requested some information, and that I was considering it, but that was last month. My mom barely listened to me."

"You should probably tell them something soon, don't you think?" Michael gave her an understanding smile. "You're a mystery, you know? You asked me to help you with the donation boxes, and I was glad to. But we haven't talked much the last two weeks. Did you notice?"

Michael had a way of pointing out the truth without making a person feel guilty, Ava thought. "Yeah, I think I noticed." She decided to be honest. "A friend of mine was giving me a hard time."

"About what?" Michael gave her plenty of time to answer.

He glanced over at the pastry counter. She sipped her mocha. Light, airy snowflakes had begun to hurry to the sidewalk.

"It's just my friend Miranda. She thinks I'm going to fall for all this religious stuff and not have any fun. Ridiculous, right?"

Ava had attended just that one meeting of Student Christian Fellowship. Miranda had talked her out of going back. And she'd given Michael an excuse that sounded legitimate at the time. *I have to get to pre-cal early for tutorials on Wednesdays.*

"I can understand what she means," Michael answered. "Reminds me of a verse in the Bible where Jesus is talking to the Jews who had believed in Him. He says, 'If you hold to my teaching, then you are really my disciples. Then you will know the truth, and the truth will set you free.'"

"Free from what?" Ava asked.

"Free from being a slave to sin. The ways of the world offer an illusion of happiness and success, but if you follow the world, in the end, you still feel empty and wanting something more."

"You said that the *truth* would set a person free from sin?" Ava asked, intently. "So what is truth?"

"Jesus Himself said, 'I am the way and the truth and the life. No one comes to the Father except through me.' Do you know what the payment for sin is, Ava?

"Yeah. A world full of chaos."

"The Bible says that the wages of sin is death. Death. But the good news is that Jesus died for our sins. He took our place. We deserved death, but he said, 'I'll pay the price.' And when we believe in his death, his resurrection, his gift of eternal life, we are free from being a slave to sin. There's just so much truth in the Bible when you read it from cover to cover. Even though God's people continually messed up, you see His plan for mankind on every page, and his plan has been redemption all along. He gave his one and only Son, Jesus Christ, and whoever believes in Him will not die, but will have everlasting life."

Michael dug in his backpack and pulled out his Bible. "Do you want to read for yourself?"

Ava scanned the coffee shop. She saw no one she knew. "Sure. Why not."

Michael scooted over to Ava's side of the table and opened his Bible to John chapter three. The two spent the next thirty minutes reading and discussing the chapter.

When they finished, Michael made a suggestion. "You should come with me Sunday to meet with my church. It's a small group. We meet in a house, so no pressure."

Ava thought about that. There might be *more* pressure in a small group. Pressure to talk. Pressure to say something. "I'll think about it."

"Okay, fair enough. I'll give you a call Saturday evening. You can let me know then," Michael offered.

"Deal. Well, should we head home before this weather gets any worse?" Ava realized she had a lot to think about. Being born again. Could it really be true? Was God speaking to her or was she falling for a lie?

Michael helped Ava slip her coat on and patted her gently on the head when she slid her hat over her ears. "Cute," he said. Pushing the door open to the freezing temperatures, he effortlessly added, "After you, my lady."

They stepped onto the busy street and bundled into the car. "So glad my Dad let me borrow the car today. Now, to take you home," Michael said.

"My parents won't be home yet. Otherwise, I'd introduce you to them," Ava told him.

"I'd love to meet them." Michael pulled onto her street. "Maybe another time."

"Yeah, my mom doesn't get home from the hotel until about six." Ava's eyes sparkled. "I just thought of a plan."

"Okay? What's your plan?" Michael pulled to the curb in front of Ava's house.

"It's top secret. I'll tell ya tomorrow! Thanks for the coffee!" With that, Ava practically ran up the sidewalk to her front door.

Quite unexpectedly, she found her dad sitting in his recliner, nodding off. Most days, he wasn't home this early at a quarter to five.

"Hey, Dad," Ava whispered. "I'm home." She sat down on the hearth opposite him.

"What's up, sweetie?" her dad responded with a yawn.

"Are you sick?" Ava asked.

"Just wasn't feeling well. I thought I'd try to beat getting sick, so I came home. No surgeries this afternoon."

"Sorry to hear that. I hope you don't get sick." Ava waited a moment. "Dad? I've been thinking. I need to get a job and earn some cash."

Mr. Zinfield sat up in bewilderment. "Whoa! Slow down, slow down. So why do you need a job so badly? You should stay focused on school right now. You've got enough going on."

"This is different, Dad. Trust me." Ava didn't know how much she wanted to say just yet. But she supposed it was now or never.

"Okay. You *know* I wanted to visit the Mercy Ship, right?

"Yes."

"You know that call the other night before dinner? It wasn't Michael. It was Mercy Ships. Several weeks ago, I requested some information about volunteering—well, that was after I found out I couldn't go for spring break," Ava confessed. "And they sent me an application, and I filled it out, and they called me. I called them back, and a lady interviewed me over the phone. She told me I'd need to raise about $3,000 for the trip—fifteen hundred for airfare plus about 800 a month, but it's actually just for six weeks, so it'll be a tiny bit less. And I already *have* about a thousand, so...."

Ava's dad cleared his throat. He didn't speak right away. Ava was glad for this. If he'd spoken right away, then she would have known he was angry. But Dad always thought through things logically, and if things made sense, that's what mattered. "Let's talk to your mom when she gets home," he offered.

Ava knew that's where she would find the most resistance. But if she could prove to them both that she was *not* buying into the religious aspect of it all, then maybe they'd be more supportive. They didn't have to know that she'd just spent the last hour at Java Cup talking with Michael about the Bible.

"This opportunity would give me such a head start on my journalism career. Just think. International travel. A chance to interview patients. Exposure to a new culture." Ava lit a candle on the coffee table.

"Sure sounds adventurous. We'll have to discuss it with your mom." Ava's dad adjusted the pillow behind his head and leaned back into his recliner.

"Okay. Get some rest, Dad. I'm going to be upstairs." Ava climbed the steps one at a time, and each step, she paused, saying in her mind. "I believe. I don't believe. I believe. I don't believe. I believe."

She reached the top. "I don't believe." *That settles it.* She'd wait for Mom to get home, and try to convince her.

CHAPTER 17

"Ava! Come help with dinner, please!"

Ava bounded down the stairs when she heard her mom calling. She started setting the table immediately.

"Dad told me you talked to him about Mercy Ships?" her mom questioned.

"Mom, I tried to tell you several weeks ago. But you just kind of ignored me. To be honest, I didn't think I'd be accepted. It's only tentative. I have to call them back and let them know for sure. It'd be for six weeks this summer— probably working in the galley. You know I *love* cooking. Just think—I could mix my culinary love with my love for words and stories and travel. What set of parents could say no to such an opportunity?" Ava excelled at persuasion.

"I just don't know, Ava." Mrs. Zinfield's furrowed brow betrayed her worry and frustration.

"I'm willing to work to earn the rest of the money I need. I'll get a job and work all spring. I'll work every Saturday and every Sunday," she added, "except when I have something extremely important to do. And Java Cup is hiring. Mom, I *really* want to do this. I think this experience could open a lot of doors." Ava decided she'd said enough.

After a few minutes, Mrs. Zinfield spoke up. "Ava, I've never seen you so passionate about something. I don't want to hold you back. If you can earn the money, you can go. You're eighteen, after all. You've grown into an amazing young woman, and I'm so proud of you. Just promise me one thing?" Her mom stopped cutting up cucumbers long enough to say, "Just keep a clear head. Don't get caught up in the emotional, religious…oh, never mind."

"I'm not, Mom. I'm not. Don't worry." Ava felt a sense of relief. She'd told her parents. They supported her. Things were falling into place.

After dinner, Ava retreated upstairs to tackle her homework. Her own words haunted her. *I'm not, Mom. I'm not.* The relief she had felt minutes before quickly turned to heaviness. She fluffed the pillows on her bed and settled in to read *1984,* required reading for English—two chapters a night. But she couldn't focus on it.

They think they're better than everyone else. She heard her dad's words echo in the stillness.

I'm sorry my mom is so judgmental. Ava winced at her mother's words to her dad. But then again, Grandma hadn't seemed judgmental when they'd visited. She seemed rather accepting. So kind. Ava felt sorry for her though.

I can't believe millions of people could be so deluded. Religion drives people to do such unreasonable things. Now it was her Grandpa Zinfield's words mocking a religious group on the news for protesting military funerals. Ava couldn't imagine Michael doing such a thing, and so there seemed to be a clear distinction between Michael and those people on TV.

Michael. Ava considered the Valentine she'd made and the meaning of Michael's name. "*Who is like God.*" And what is Michael like? Ava answered her own question. *He's friendly. He sticks up for you. He's patient. He doesn't bring up the times you denied him to save your reputation. He buys you gift cards to Java Cup on Valentine's Day. Oh, Ava snap out of it!*

Ava flipped on her radio to the classical music station and picked up *1984* once more. Got to get it done. She picked up where she'd left off.

Poor Winston, Ava thought. O'Brien held up four fingers and asked Winston to tell him how many he was holding up. Winston clearly saw four, but O'Brien would take nothing less than five for an answer, so Winston yelled five. But that answer wasn't accepted either because O'Brien could tell that Winston still *thought* there were four. Ava snapped the book closed. The government was telling him one thing—that there were five fingers, when he only saw four. She sympathized with Winston. So many voices in Ava's mind said that there was no God. But that day after journalism, after looking up the meaning of Michael's name, Ava had certainly felt something different. Was she deceiving herself? How could she be sure of anything?

The Bible that Grandma and Grandpa Coetzee sent her had remained untouched on the bookshelf on the far side of her room. Ava recalled sitting in Grandpa Amery's recliner and opening his Bible on Christmas morning. What was the story she'd read? *A woman named Mary had broken expensive perfume on Jesus' feet. Jesus had raised a man from the dead. And Judas had said the perfume should have been sold and given to the poor. Sounds like a good plan. Give to the poor. That's the mission of Mercy Ships. To bring hope and healing to the poor. Is that why I want to go?*

She opened the sea-colored Bible—her name in gold on the front—toward the beginning and scanned the pages for what, she didn't know. Hard-to-pronounce names and unfamiliar places. That's all that caught her eye. Places of long ago. People of long ago. Nephtoah. Ephron. Achor. The wilderness of Zin. Not relevant. A mere history book. She closed the Bible and placed it back on the shelf.

Her heart still felt heavy. She forced herself to finish reading the assigned chapters in *1984* and went downstairs to watch TV, the perfect distraction from all this thinking.

CHAPTER 18

February 16, 2006

Hello Ava!

You applied to Mercy Ships? HOW EXCITING!! I hope you get to come this summer. I know you'd absolutely love it, and you could even meet the kids at the orphanage. How cool would that be? By then, they'll be building the new dorms. By the way, I love your picture idea. I can't wait to see it.

The dream you had—I really have been praying for you. One Thursday night at our community meeting, I felt overwhelmed to pray for you. It was January 12. I marked it down on my calendar because it seemed so significant. Remember some of the others you met on the beach that day? Elise and Sophie were praying with me, too. I thought you might like to know that. I wonder if we were praying for you the same night you had that dream.

The Bible tells of Jesus healing many people who were blind—some who were physically blind, and some who were spiritually blind. I think of the story of the blind beggar Bartimaeus in Mark 10:46-52. He called out to Jesus even when those around him were telling him to be quiet. Jesus came to him and asked what he could do for him. Bartimaeus said, "Rabbi, I want to see." Jesus told him that his faith had healed him, and immediately he could see, and he followed Jesus along the road.

So how did I become a Christian? It might sound strange, but I realized I was blind. Spiritually blind. I realized that I had sin in my heart and that the only way I could be connected to God was through accepting that Jesus died to pay for my sins on the cross. Before Jesus lived on earth, God's people sacrificed animals and sprinkled the blood on the altar in the tabernacle as a payment for their sins. They did this because

God told them to. For without blood, God said there would be no forgiveness of sin. But it was just a foreshadowing of what was to come. Because then Jesus came and shed his own blood as a payment for sin. Hebrews 9:22 says, "How much more, then, will the blood of Christ, who through the eternal Spirit offered himself unblemished to God, cleanse our consciences from acts that lead to death, so that we may serve the living God!"

I was eleven when I finally understood this, and I remember coming home from church one evening, kneeling by my bed, and telling God that I wanted to follow Him and His ways. I told him that I accepted his forgiveness and that I believed he had died for my sins and that I wanted to live this new life he offered. Read Romans 10: 9-10: "If you declare with your mouth, "Jesus is Lord," and believe in your heart that God raised him from the dead, you will be saved. For it is with your heart that you believe and are justified, and it is with your mouth that you profess your faith and are saved."

Start reading the book of John in the New Testament. And send me your questions. I'm so excited about what God is doing in your life. There's so much more we can talk about.

To answer your last question, school ends on the 9th of June. I'll have to stay another few weeks on board until my dad is finished with surgeries, so I'm on the ship until the end of June. Then we'll spend all of July and half of August at my grandparents' place in Virginia. Of course, we'll do some traveling, but that will be our home base for a month and a half. Then I start my senior year at the beginning of September in a new country. Ghana! That's where the ship will be next. I know you're busy. Write when you can.

Sending sunshine,

—Jessie

March 3, 2006

Hey Jessie!

Here's the picture! About fifty people showed up. But I'm sure more people must have donated because we received just over $500 dollars! I'll wire it to you tomorrow. So... I've given Mercy Ships a definite answer. YES! I'm coming. Now for all the immunizations. Yellow fever? Yikes! Hepatitis A and B. Help! I'll be fine though. No worries.

So much has been happening. Sorry that I haven't written sooner. I graduate June 16, so I will leave that next week for Liberia, as soon as the following Monday, June 19th. I can't believe it! Can you?

I got a job at Java Cup, and I work three four-hour shifts after school during the week and at least one eight-hour shift on the weekends. If my math is right, I could earn about $1,800 this spring if I save every penny. I'll be working every day during spring break. When I told the manager my plan to serve with Mercy Ships this summer, she was very impressed and said she'd do whatever she could to make sure I got the shifts I needed. I told her all about touring the ship in South Africa, and she was impressed that I wanted to volunteer. I never thought it'd be so much fun to learn how to make all the different coffees. I love working at Java Cup! And it's for a good cause!

You'll be glad to know that I've read one chapter of John. My friend Michael read it with me, but I've been so busy with homework, working at Java Cup, and planning for this summer and college, I haven't read any more. I'll let you know if I have any questions.

Sending more snow! —-Ava

The spring weeks flew by as Ava tackled pre-cal, pumpkin lattes, and fragile friendships. She enjoyed writing to Jessie and asked every question she could think of to get ready for her departure to Mercy

Ships. But she didn't ask any questions about the Bible. Talking about real, tangible things proved much easier.

If she could just keep Miranda satisfied. Why did she even try? She had thought she'd let herself have some fun. She had trusted Miranda. But nothing had turned out like she'd planned. The party *had* been fun—for the first hour or so. Things quickly got out of hand, though, and Ava called her dad and asked him to come pick her up. The next day, she'd found out that the police had been called to the "party" house. She'd heard countless stories of parties gone wrong, and she was almost a part of one. She had no intentions of ruining her good reputation. At least her work at Java Cup gave her an excuse to say no to most of Miranda's wild, senior-year offers for fun.

Prom was approaching, and even though Ava had bought a dress, she didn't have a date, and she wasn't as excited about the big event as she thought she would be. Miranda was going with Brett, so going with her was not an option, and it was already the first week in April. She had initiated a conversation with Michael about the big event, but Michael had made it clear that he didn't plan to go.

"I don't know most of the people here," Michael had told her, "and besides, prom isn't quite my style."

"What *is* your style then?" Ava asked him.

"I'll let you know when I figure it out," Michael said. "Anyway, I already have plans that Saturday."

"Oh? And what plans might those be?" Ava asked.

"It's my grandma's 60th birthday. We've been planning a big celebration, not only for her birthday, but for the end of her cancer treatment."

"How big of a celebration? She's in remission?" Ava asked.

"Maybe fifty people? Not sure. She has a pretty big church family. And yes, the cancer is gone for now." Michael smiled.

Ava brought to mind the church service in South Africa and questioned whether the people there were also like a big family. She felt so confused. So conflicted. Religion had divided her own family, and now complete strangers were coming together because of it. She thought that, if there were a God, he had spoken to her, right there in the bathroom stall. She knew what she had felt that Valentine's Day, but she'd pushed all those feelings deep down inside. After all, would those closest to her understand? Would they laugh at her if she said she believed? What would they think of her? Would they take her seriously? She didn't want to be seen as "one of those Christians."

If they only knew what I know, they wouldn't laugh. But what do I know? I know that...that...that. Do I know anything?

The Monday before spring break, Ava made a trip to the library at school for a new book. No sooner had she started to look, Michael appeared.

"Why don't you come back to Student Christian Fellowship, Ava?" he asked her as she scanned the shelf for books.

"I just can't," Ava had told him.

"Just be honest and tell me why. That one day at lunch, when you gave me the Valentine, something was going on. Why were you crying?" Michael gently pressed for an answer.

Ava was silent. "Michael. I think it's fine if you want to believe. For a moment, even I thought God was speaking to me. But what if it's all just coincidence?"

As she scanned the rows of books, and as Michael patiently waited, she thought of Grandma Coetzee—how she'd cried out to God, and how she'd heard a knock at her door almost immediately. And Grandma Coeztee had even said she'd prayed for her, that she'd have a "personal" experience just like she'd had.

"But how many times have people cried out to God, and *nothing* happened? Nothing." Ava turned from the books and glared at Michael, demanding an answer.

"Whoa. Where did that come from?" Michael asked her.

"I'm sorry I sounded angry. It's just that... like I said, it's fine that you believe. It's good. Keep it up."

"Okay. I understand. See you tomorrow morning? SCF? Seven thirty. We'll be expecting you." Michael selected a book from the shelf and held it out to her. "And I recommend this one."

Ava squinted at the spine. *Les Miserables*. "You've read this?"

"Yep. See you tomorrow, I hope. I gotta go, or I'll be late," he said, rushing off. The thought crossed Ava's mind that perhaps Michael had seen her in the library and come there just to talk to her. One thing seemed certain. He wasn't giving up.

April 12, 2006

Dear Ava,

Hey, girl! Time is going so fast. I can't believe you're really coming! I'm looking forward to having you on the ship for two weeks. I know you'll be working...and no doubt, you'll do some reporting from the field, but I sure hope there's time left to hang out.

So... Easter is coming up this weekend. What do you usually do for Easter? We'll have a special Passover meal here on the ship on Good Friday and a big celebration service on Easter morning. On Saturday, it's our team's turn to go to the orphanage, and we'll be telling the Easter story with a dozen plastic Easter eggs, each filled with a tiny object to help tell the story. I wish you could be there to see it. But maybe you can, after all. I'll video it and send it to you via e-mail. I don't know why I didn't think of this before.

Talk soon. —-Jessie

April 13, 2006

Hi, Jessie. Thanks for the news from the ship. To answer your question about Easter, the only thing we do anymore to celebrate is eat out with my grandpa. When I was little, my parents would take me to the Forest Hills Playground nearby for the neighborhood Easter egg hunt. I always loved wearing cute little dresses. It sounds like Easter is a big deal on the ship.

I was going to go to Christian Student Fellowship yesterday, but right when I got to school, my friend Miranda had an "emergency" and said she needed my help with pre-cal home-work. We have pre-cal together first period.

Who knows? Maybe I'll go to church on Sunday. I've never been to an Easter service, but I think I'd like it very much. Talk soon! Can't wait until this summer! Ciao! —-Ava

Ava hit send. *Why did I tell her I might go to church on Sunday? Where would I even go? I can help people without getting caught up in all this religious stuff. Besides, I can't tell my parents I'm going to church. And what about Miranda?*

CHAPTER 19

Good Friday came and went. Ava had not shown up for SCF, and Michael never mentioned that he'd missed her. Of course, she'd very purposefully managed to ignore him the rest of the week. Not the mean kind of ignore. Just the "I'm-really-busy" type of ignore, which couldn't be taken as an offense.

On Saturday night, Ava worked the late shift at Java Cup. Her mind was thankfully filled with lattes and mochas and green teas instead of Easter morning. There were no more childish traditions now that she was grown, just eating with Grandpa Zinfield at some fancy restaurant. Mom had always said Easter was her break from cooking.

Her shift ended at 11, and her dad had agreed to pick her up so she wouldn't be out alone so late. Apron and hat tucked under her arm, she swung her purse over her shoulder. On the way out, she stopped to check the bulletin board above the coffee station. She'd seen a young man posting something earlier, and although she hated to admit it, she was curious. The word *church* had caught her eye.

Join Restoration Church for Easter services, April 16, 2006, 10:30 AM at Woodrow Wilson High School, Atrium.

Seriously? They're having church in my school? Since when? How could this be?

Ava tried to imagine what a church service would be like in the atrium of Wilson High as she stepped out into the chilly spring night to meet her dad.

"Hey, Ava," her dad greeted her when she got in the car. "How was your shift?"

"Busy, busy, busy. I'm exhausted." Ava was wondering what excuse she could make up to go to the school tomorrow. But there was no good excuse. No school scheduled anything on an Easter Sunday.

If she were going to go to church, she'd just have to tell her parents the truth. After all, she would have to borrow one of their cars.

Hopefully, she'd get her own car for graduation. Maybe that would be *one* thing she wouldn't have to save up for.

"Hey, Dad. Are we eating with Grandpa tomorrow for Easter?" Ava asked.

"Yes, we are. Italian this time. Probably around 1 o'clock," he answered.

"Well, I need to get in some research before I join Mercy Ships this summer. There's a lady I need to meet with tomorrow at the school. I know it sounds crazy, but there's a church that's having an Easter service at the school, and this lady is going to be there." Ava thought quickly. "She came in Java Cup today wearing a Mercy Ships' shirt, so I asked her a few questions, and I found out that she volunteered with Mercy Ships a few years ago. When I told her I was going this summer, she invited me to come to church so we could talk about it more. It would be fun to interview her and ask her about her experiences. I'll be done by one for sure. So, I was just wondering if I could borrow the car." Ava tried to sound as factual as possible.

She was amazed at how natural the lie sounded. But this lie was *necessary*. It would prevent her parents from any unnecessary stress. Yes, that was it.

"I'm sure you can borrow the car," her dad said, hesitantly. Ava felt as if her dad wanted to say something, but held his tongue.

She was just thankful she'd come up with a good reason to go. So it was settled. She'd go to church on Easter Sunday. How hard could that be? Then she could tell Jessie all about it and sound educated about religious things. After all, Jessie had encouraged her to read the book of John in the Bible, and she still hadn't done so—except for chapter three, which she'd read with Michael at Java Cup. The contents of that chapter still came to mind from time to time as she went through her days, but she tried not to think about it too much. Being born again. Eternal life. Things that seemed distant and so very intangible. Jessie would probably ask her whether she had gone to church, and Ava didn't want to disappoint her. At least, that's what she told herself. But there was something deeper stirring inside her that she couldn't quite put into words.

The next morning, Ava rummaged through her closet for something to wear to church. She decided on her new dark jeans and a deep satiny-blue blouse.

"Mom, I'll be back before one. Shouldn't take too long. I just want to get this interview done." Ava played out the lie. But inside her purse, she stashed the sea-colored Bible, along with her writer's notebook for the "interview."

"Okay, sweetie. Be careful. I'm glad it's at the school. At least you're familiar with the place," she teased, handing Ava the car keys.

Ava found a parking spot near the entrance. It was 10:20. From her experience at church in South Africa, she thought she knew what to expect. She entered the front doors of her school and instead of the shuffle and chatter of a few hundred teenagers, a melodic tune from a keyboard resounded throughout the atrium.

A woman with a box full of carnations greeted her. "Welcome! Take one, please."

Ava didn't expect this. Maybe she didn't know what to expect after all. She chose a red carnation and headed toward the chairs set up in the atrium of the school, wondering if flowers were part of every Sunday service. She found a seat and just tried to be inconspicuous. She cut her eyes to her right. *Isn't that Sarah?*

Sarah was in her government class last period, and earlier this year, they'd been partners for a project. *She's a Christian? I would have never guessed. She's always bragging about some party she's been to. One more reason none of this is true. What difference does it make? Just be good for goodness sake.*

Now Ava wanted to leave. She could walk out just as easily as she'd walked in. She focused her attention straight ahead at a white cross of lattice, centered in front, and decided to just go through with it. She reached in her purse to appear busy. Where was her lip gloss?

"Hey, Ava." Ava nearly jumped from her seat.

She hadn't seen Sarah approach.

"Hey, Sarah. I didn't expect to see you here," Ava told her. At least that was the truth.

"Yeah, my grandma *made* me come," Sarah moaned. "I would have rather stayed home. I'm surprised to see you, too." Sarah smiled a knowing smile. "Wanna sit together?"

"Sure." Ava wasn't so sure, but it was too late. The service was starting.

"Let's all stand and sing, shall we?" the man in front encouraged them. "And as we sing, starting with the first row, we'll come and place our flowers on the cross, as a symbol of joy that Christ is risen!"

In unison, the congregation responded, "He is risen indeed!"

Three singers stood at the mikes in the front and the music started. "Hallelujah! Jesus is alive. Death has lost its victory, and the grave has been denied," they sang.

The first row started toward the cross. One woman started dancing toward it. Already, tears streamed down her face, and she knelt, placing her flower between one of the latticed openings in the very middle.

The cross was filling with carnations of white and red—such a beautiful thing to see. Soon enough, Ava's row headed toward the cross. Sarah was first. She placed her white flower nonchalantly in one of the open spaces and headed back toward her seat.

Ava paused. *God? Show me truth, please. I'm asking you. If you're really out there.* She placed her red carnation in the same section the dancing lady had placed hers and followed Sarah back to their row.

After several more songs, the pastor stood up and asked for those giving testimonies to come forward.

Testimonies? Ava leaned forward, eager to hear, searching for answers.

The dancing lady was first. "I praise God that he delivered me from depression. I praise God that he met me at my lowest point and walked with me through the many years of struggle and pain. And because Jesus is alive, I can live an abundant life!"

The man standing next to her followed. "My life was spiraling down fast. I was up to no good, dabbling with drugs, lying to my parents and telling them I was fine. I lost my job. I lost my apartment. A friend let me live with him for a while, but then he kicked me out. I ended up in a shelter. That's where I heard the message of salvation. And now, praise God, I am alive in Christ!"

The lie Ava had told her parents started to feel a bit uncomfortable as people shared about their own failings. Several more testimonies followed, and it seemed that most of the people who had spoken had made bad choices. In comparison, Ava was still pretty good... for goodness sake. Maybe this scene wasn't for her.

The minister made his way to the podium to speak.

"Open your Bibles to Matthew 28," he began.

Ava reached in her purse for her Bible. She could still almost feel the softness of that Christmas morning as she sat in Grandpa's recliner, wrapped in the sea-colored robe. Grandma knew it was her favorite color.

Ava fumbled to the table of contents.

"Here, I'll help." Sarah reached over and flipped right to Matthew. "I was forced to come to church as a child. I can recite all the books of the Bible," she whispered, smiling.

Forced? I came of my own free will, Ava thought.

Sarah dug through her purse. Ava followed along as the pastor began reading:

After the Sabbath, at dawn on the first day of the week, Mary Magdalene and the other Mary went to look at the tomb. There was a violent earthquake, for an angel of the Lord came down from heaven and, going to the tomb, rolled back the stone and sat on it. His appearance was like lightning, and his clothes were white as snow. The guards were so afraid of him that they shook and became like dead men. The angel said to the women, "Do not be afraid, for I know that you are looking for Jesus, who was crucified. He is not here; he has risen, just as he said. Come and see the place where he lay."

The pastor read the entire chapter. Ava learned that soldiers who had been guarding Jesus' tomb ran to tell the chief priests and elders that his body was gone. But the leaders paid the soldiers a great deal of money to spread a lie and to report that Jesus' own disciples had come to steal his body in order to make it seem as though he'd risen from the dead.

Lies. Lies. Lies. And who knew the truth? The disciples had seen Jesus after he'd risen from the dead. But the soldiers had lied for money to cover up the truth that he arose. Ava, there you go again. Mom warned you about this, remember?

As Ava listened to the pastor, her thoughts wandered from Rock Creek Park, to meeting Michael, to Boulder's Beach in South Africa, to Christmas morning and the meaning of Michael's name.

"And so if you would like this new life in Christ, you can have it today," she heard the minister say. "Are you doubting, like some of the disciples who saw Jesus after he arose? Jesus understands."

"The kingdom of heaven is like treasure hidden in a field. When a man found it, he hid it again, and then in his joy went and sold all he had and bought that field. Again, the kingdom of heaven is like a merchant looking for fine pearls. When he found one of great value, he went away and sold everything he had and bought it," the pastor read from Matthew 13.

"Who is that man seeking a treasure? Who is the merchant seeking the pearl? Is it not Christ? The Bible says that Jesus has come to seek and save the lost. Is He seeking you today? Are you seeking him? In a moment, you'll have a chance to come and talk with someone if you'd like to have new life today."

Ava heard the words, but her in her mind, she was on the cliffs of Cape Point, posing in a photo with her mom and grandma, who held forth the other two pearls that Grandpa Zinfield had found. It seemed like a dream. *Pearls. A pearl of great price. He came to save the lost.*

Ava stood with everyone else. Someone walked down to the front. Ava couldn't and wouldn't move from her seat. *What did he say about the pearl of great price? Grandma wrote that in my Bible. She said I was a pearl of great price. Is that what she meant? Am I that precious to God? Is He really seeking me?*

Ava reached for her necklace, a gift from her grandfather who was killed before she was ever born, when her mother was only seven.

Come on, Ava. You don't have time for this religious stuff. This is not who you are. Life is beautiful. Live your life. Let other people live theirs. Just be accepting. This experience is to help you be more accepting of people, to help you see that the people here are not crazy. They're just good... for a different reason.

The service ended. Ava quickly said goodbye to Sarah and headed straight for the exit. She'd be glad to come back to school on Monday to go to pre-cal, where answers to problems seemed much more attainable. No time to talk to anyone. Besides, she needed to meet her parents and her grandpa for Easter lunch, and she didn't want to be late.

A silver-haired woman wearing a purple blazer was positioned at the door, shaking hands with the Easter morning church-goers. A young couple slipped past the woman, and Ava followed right behind them. She dashed out the door and headed for her car. She'd only taken a few steps in that direction when she heard a voice behind her.

"Hello? Young lady in the blue. Excuse me. May I speak to you for one moment?"

Ava froze and turned to look. It was the silver-haired woman. She had left her post at the door and was coming to meet her. Why had this woman singled her out?

"First time here?" she asked.

"Uhm, yeah, first time. I mean, I go to school here, so no, but yes. First time to come to church here."

The silver-haired woman spoke. "Ever since you came in, I've been praying for you. And I genuinely feel like God would have me give you this to show you His love, and I see that it would look lovely with your necklace."

The woman removed a small pin from her lapel. One pearl sat securely surrounded by tiny diamonds. "May I?" With wrinkled hands, she pinned the jewel onto the collar of Ava's deep blue, satiny blouse. "You *are* a precious pearl. And God wants you to know that."

Ava was speechless. "Thank you, thank you. I don't know what to say. Thank you, again. You have no idea how much this means."

"Come back and visit us," the woman told her.

"Maybe I will," Ava said. She hurried out the door before the tears could fall. *How is God doing this? It's like he's speaking right to me!*

CHAPTER 20

Grandpa Zinfield was waiting in the lobby of the restaurant when Ava and her parents arrived. "So I hear you're going on a ship this summer, is that right, Ava?"

"Sure is! I'll get a taste of reporting from the field, and I'll get to travel. I've been working at Java Cup to earn my own money to go. And I'm hoping Dad will go ahead and get me a car for graduation since I've been such a hard-working daughter." Ava smiled and leaned on her dad, teasing him. She hoped no one could tell she'd been crying.

"It's a Christian ship," Ava's Dad volunteered.

Ava felt her face flush. This was the moment she dreaded. What would they think of her if she told them all that was in her heart? Why did dad have to say anything?

The hostess led them to their table, and everyone ordered their favorites. Ava knew that the talk would center around her, so she tried to ask questions.

"So, Grandpa, what's been keeping you busy these days?" she asked.

"Let's see... I've been writing a few things here and there....and gardening. You'll have to come over and help me soon," Grandpa Zinfield said. "Why, that's a pretty pearl pin you've got there. It matches your necklace quite well."

"Where did you get *that*, Ava?" her mom asked. "It's beautiful!"

"The lady I interviewed at church—she gave it to me," Ava told them. "It's not real," Ava added, to dispel attention from the pearl that seemed to be burning a hole in her collar. "It's just a thank you for interviewing her." She wished she had thought to take it off.

Satisfied with that answer, her dad changed the subject and started talking golf with Grandpa. And her mom started quizzing her on colleges. Dinner was over by two o'clock, and everyone headed home. Ava was thankful no one asked her anything about church.

Safely tucked away in her room, Ava pulled out her laptop, an early graduation present from her parents. She opened her e-mail, desperate to write to someone she knew would understand. To Ava's relief, there was an e-mail from Jessie. She opened it and saw an attachment. Just as she'd promised—the video.

As a child, Ava remembered hunting Easter eggs in the perfectly landscaped community park of her D.C. neighborhood. The fancy dresses, cute wicker baskets, and cuddly bunnies.

Ava opened the video and leaned back on her pillows to watch.

Beneath a tree, about fifty children crowded onto a blue tarp that was spread on the bare dusty ground surrounding the cinder-block orphanage.

"Today, we're going to tell the Easter story using something very special. And we'll need some volunteers." Hands shot up all over the group of children gathered onto the tarp.

Mrs. Landers, the academy principal whom Jessie had met that day while touring the ship, quickly calmed the children into a tightly-packed, attentive group, eager to see what each egg held inside. "I need a very brave volunteer to come open the first egg," she told the children.

Little Jo Jo was chosen first. She cracked open the purple egg and pulled out a tiny green branch that looked like the branch from a palm tree.

"When Jesus came into Jerusalem on Friday, the people waved palm branches and shouted, 'Hosanna! Blessed is He who comes in the name of the Lord!' Everyone, say that with me on the count of three," Mrs. Landers directed the group.

Everyone followed her command and the sound of fifty little voices chimed in unison.

"The people were so excited that Jesus was in their town. They thought he had come to be their ruler, their leader. They spread their cloaks and their palm branches on the ground as He rode into Jerusalem on a donkey."

A little boy named Reuben opened egg number two. The silver coins inside fell to the ground with a jangle as he fumbled with the egg. She picked up the coins and handed them back to Reuben. Jessie was there in the front row, a child on her lap. She turned to the camera and waved, mouthing, "Hello, Ava."

Mrs. Landers continued, "After Jesus came into Jerusalem and had a meal with his disciples, one of those disciples named Judas betrayed him. Judas told the leaders of the city where they could find Jesus, and in return, the leaders gave Judas thirty pieces of silver. The leaders of the city wanted to arrest Jesus because they thought he was going to try to be king. And then they would no longer have positions of leadership."

Ava pondered the fact that Judas had also accused Mary of wasting her perfume by pouring it on Jesus' feet.

Comfort, a shy-looking toddler, came and opened the next egg to reveal a tiny pair of praying hands, and Mrs. Landers explained their significance. "Jesus took some of his disciples to the garden to pray with him. He knew that he would soon be killed on the cross, and He prayed, 'Father, not my will, but thy will be done.'"

Suddenly, Ava remembered her dream of being on the operating table while Jessie prayed for her. She paused the video. *Had* Jessie prayed for her the same day she'd had that dream? She'd never found out. *It was the same day I applied to Mercy Ships at school. The same day I started that article.* Ava opened some e-mails from Jessie searching for some evidence. She scanned through a few e-mails and found what she was looking for. Her own words jumped off the screen.

I'll write more later. I gotta get to work on this article about the Mercy Ship—I'm writing to you in my journalism class, but I have permission, don't worry. You're an important part of my research. I'm going to check out the Mercy Ships' website now and get some info from there...

Yes, that was the day. Ava checked the date of the e-mail again. January 12. It *was* the same day. But not the same time, Ava thought, trying to brush off the significance of the date. Her eyes fell on the red digits of her alarm clock. *There's a time difference.* She ran a search. *Time difference between Washington D.C. and Monrovia, Liberia.* She stared at the result that came back. Four hours' difference. *If I had the dream at four in the afternoon, it would have been eight o'clock Jessie's time, right in the middle of their community meeting.* Ava could feel her throat tighten uncomfortably. She resumed the video.

A girl named Peace opened the fourth egg. Ava did not miss the irony. "While Jesus was praying in the garden, the soldiers came to arrest him. Then they took him before the leaders who beat him with leather whips like these."

Prince opened egg five and hollered, "Ouch!" He held up the thorny stem of a plant. "The soldiers pressed a crown of thorns on Jesus' head," Mrs. Landers told the children. Then she pointed out the various trials Jesus was put through and how ultimately, he was nailed to the cross. The people had a choice to release a murderer, Barabbas, or Jesus, who had claimed to be the Son of God. The people yelled that Barabbas should be released. And what about Jesus? *"Crucify Him!" the people yelled.*

Eggs six and seven held the cross and the nails. Egg eight held dice. "After Jesus died on the cross, the soldiers gambled for his clothes," Mrs. Landers explained.

With the opening of egg nine, Ava learned that a man named Joseph asked for Jesus' body and wrapped it in linen and laid it in a tomb. Egg ten held a cotton ball that smelled like perfume. Jesus' body was anointed with spices and oils.

Egg eleven held one smooth stone, which represented the stone rolled in front of the tomb. "Soldiers guarded the tomb day and night, so that no one would come and steal Jesus' body and claim that he had risen from the dead." Mrs. Landers had the children's complete attention.

Yes! That's right! I learned that in church today.

For a moment, Ava was sitting cross-legged on the blue tarp with Jessie. Did all these children believe that Jesus died for them—for their sins? If they did believe, what difference did it make in their lives? They would still grow up without parents, with limited opportunities, without hope for a better life. Wouldn't they?

Mrs. Landers held forth the last egg. Mercy, the girl on Jessie's lap, was chosen to stand up in front of the group to reveal its contents. When she cracked it open, her eyes got wide and she stomped her foot, "Mine doesn't have anything in it!"

"Exactly! When the women came to the tomb early on Sunday morning, Easter morning, Jesus was not there! He had risen, just like He said." Mrs. Landers added, "Because Jesus is alive, you can be alive. You can put your trust in Him, believing He died for your sins."

The children were getting restless, especially after laughing at Mercy's outburst, so Mrs. Landers had them stand to sing. Jo Jo, the girl who had opened the first egg, stepped in front of the group. She started clapping and the other children followed her lead. She sang loud and strong all by herself: *Hallelujah! Glory be to God.* The other children echoed her.

Hallelujah! Glory be to God. Clap, clap, clap!

When the song was over, Jessie spoke to the children, "Everyone, look at the camera and wave hello to my friend, Ava, in the United States."

The children put on a show, laughing and jostling for a place in the front near the camera. "Hello! Hello!" they cried out. They waved and jumped up and down as if they knew her, as if she were right there. With such joy they smiled!

The video was over. Ava stared at the computer screen blurry with the faces of children, frozen on screen. She picked up the phone. There was someone she had to call. *Michael.*

CHAPTER 21

"Hello, Michael. Can we talk? I have some questions…. now is fine, or we can meet at Java Cup this evening, if you're not busy. You think you can meet me there? Yes, I'm okay. I just need to talk. Okay, see you at seven."

Ava arrived early and got a seat in the corner. How often she had watched people come and go throughout the spring, talking and laughing, figuring things out over a cup of coffee or tea, sometimes even crying and praying. Yes, she had seen that, too. And somehow that was comforting to remember now.

"Hey, there, Ava." Michael slid into the seat across from her. "So, what can I get you?"

"Oh, hey! Thanks for coming. Chai tea latte?" Ava requested.

Ava walked to the counter with Michael. "I wasn't suggesting you had to buy, silly."

"No, don't even think of it. My treat. So….you have some questions?"

"Yeah. But first let me tell you what happened today. I know you invited me to church. Sorry I didn't go with you, but I *did* go."

"You did? Where?"

"At school. Can you believe it? Did you know that a church started meeting there on Sundays?"

"Yeah, I think I had heard that. So you went? Sweet!" Michael ordered their drinks, and then leaned on the counter and waited for Ava to continue. "So what happened?"

"It was the most amazing thing. The pastor was saying that heaven was like a merchant looking for pearls, and when he finds one of great value, he goes and sells everything he has to buy that pearl. As I was leaving, a lady stopped me at the door and said she'd been praying for me the whole service. Then she gave me this pearl pendant and said I was a precious pearl and that God *really* wanted me to know that." Ava said the words slowly, her voice filled with unshed tears.

"That's awesome!" Michael smiled.

"No, you don't understand. My grandmother from South Africa sent me a Bible, and on the inside she wrote, 'To Ava, a pearl of great price.' And see this necklace? My grandfather *found* this pearl and reserved it for me before I was even born."

Ava took a sip of her chai tea. "Can you explain that?" she asked Michael as they returned to their seats. "Is this coincidence? Or is this God speaking to me?"

"Surely, I would be biased, right? Of course I think it's God speaking to you. He's pretty good at speaking to us if we are listening. He did create the universe, you know," Michael said with his winsome smile.

"What if people created God?" Ava quipped back, the tears gone from her voice. "What if all of these coincidences are just that—coincidences—and people just attribute them to a supernatural force they call God because they can't explain them.

"People didn't create God, Ava. He created us. Look around you. Would you ever say that this coffee shop just appeared one day out of the blue? Of course you wouldn't. People designed it, planned it, built it, invested in it, and now they maintain it every day. Now look at us." Michael held out his hands. "We're so much more complicated than a coffee shop. There's not a chance that we didn't have a designer."

"It just goes against *reason*," Ava argued.

"No, it goes *with* reason. It's reasonable to believe that someone created us and loves us and redeemed us. And now, instead of forcing us to believe it, He gives us a choice to believe. To trust. To live. To really live."

"But I've been *good* my whole life. I'm a good person. Why can't other people just be good for goodness' sake, not just because there is a God waiting to punish us?" Ava felt her arguments crumbling.

"Well, first of all, the punishment has already been taken. So God is not wanting to punish us. The Bible says, 'For God made Christ, who never sinned, to be the offering for our sin, so that we could be made right with God through Christ.'"

"Okay, so you're quoting from a book that was written by men and may not even be accurate. How can we even know the Bible is true? Didn't regular men write the Bible? Sounds like there's a lot of room for error, to me." Ava used an argument she'd heard her dad use successfully many times.

"It's true that the Bible is a collection of many writers' records of history, but these writers were inspired by the Holy Spirit." Michael sipped his mocha. "Ava, there's so much in the Bible that completely makes sense when you consider it all together, from Genesis to Revelation. There's so much I have yet to discover for myself in the Bible. But I know the one most important thing."

"Just one thing, huh? What's that one thing?" Ava asked sincerely.

"God has made a way, and it's free for the taking," Michael said.

"A way for what?"

"A way to be right with God. A way to have life, and have it abundantly."

"And how do I get that life?" Ava wasn't sure she was ready.

"Accept that Jesus paid it all for you. Trusting in your own good-ness... or believing that you've messed up so bad that God can't save you... that's all from the enemy. No one is good enough. And no one is beyond God's reach. Jesus said, 'Whoever believes in him who sent me has eternal life. He does not come into judgment but has passed from death to life.' You see, when we choose to follow him we become new creations."

"How do you explain the ark?" Ava demanded. My grandma gave me a children's Bible, and on the front is a picture of the ark, which supposedly Noah built when the world was flooded. And... I just don't see how it's possible that two of *every* animal could fit on the ark, and the *entire* world was flooded? And only Noah and his family were saved? What kind of God would inflict that kind of pun-ishment on people that he supposedly loved? That kind of thing just doesn't make any sense to me."

"A lot of things don't exactly make sense to me, either, Ava. But the Bible says that the earth was corrupt and full of violence. And yes, He sent the flood to cover the earth, but he made a covenant, or a promise, that he would never again flood the earth. Do you know what the sign of that promise is?"

"I have no clue," Ava admitted.

"A rainbow."

Ava was caught off-guard. "Seriously? Now you're going to bring up rainbows?" She stared out the window, averting her eyes from Michael, recalling the beautiful rainbow she'd seen when she stepped off the ship in Cape Town after the tour of the Mercy Ship *Anastasis*.

Ava had seen plenty of rainbows in her lifetime, but this was the first time she paused to consider the significance of one.

"Rainbows can be explained scientifically," Ava said after a minute.

"Of course they can," Michael shot back. "God created science." Michael was quiet for a moment. "Tell me what you're thinking," he said.

Ava didn't speak right away. "I saw a rainbow in Cape Town when my dad and I stepped off the ship after the tour."

"Tell me more," Michael encouraged her.

"The rainbow seemed to be shooting right out of this mountain called Lion's Head, which I think my grandpa said was an ancient volcano." Ava paused a moment. "Just a rainbow."

"Intriguing," Michael said, smiling.

"What? What are you smiling about?" Ava asked him, a little annoyed.

"I was just thinking, that's all. Jesus is referred to as the *Lion* of Judah."

"Uhm, okay." Ava was remembering. There was Devil's Peak and Lion's Head. Inside, her heart was bursting, but she didn't want to be emotional. Not now. "I need to think about all this. Can we talk about something else? College? Anything? What are your plans for the summer?"

Michael obliged and talked easily about all his summer plans until they'd taken their last sips.

"I should get home," Ava said.

"Are you sure you don't have any more questions?"

"Not tonight. Thanks for meeting me." Ava had also wanted to tell him about the dream, but something stopped her. It was too much.

"Anytime," Michael told her.

The evening air was cool and crisp when they left Java Cup. Michael rested his hand on Ava's head as he opened the door. "After you, my lady." It was becoming his signature goodbye.

Ava couldn't help but smile at his gesture. "Thanks again for meeting me, Michael. I mean, thanks for listening and sharing."

"Like I said, anytime." Michael tucked his hands in his pockets.

"See you at school tomorrow," Ava called as she waved, heading toward the car. As soon as she got in and shut the door, the tears broke through.

And all the way home, she thought of the rainbow.

CHAPTER 22

Ava had never felt so relieved as when the plane's wheels hit the ground at the airport in Monrovia, Liberia. Terrified of navigating an airport in a foreign country, she desperately hoped that Jessie would be among the Mercy Ships' crew who had arranged to welcome her and pick her up from the airport.

April, May, and June had flown by in a dizziness of prom talk, final exams, and graduation. Her much-anticipated trip to serve with Mercy Ships was finally a reality.

Perhaps Jessie had watched her plane land. Jessie had said she'd come with whoever was assigned to pick her up. She'd have a sign with her name, but Ava knew she wouldn't need a sign as long as Jessie was there.

Ava carefully stepped down the plane's stairs which descended all the way to the solid ground of Liberia and cupped her hand over her mouth and nose. She untied her light summer jacket from her waist and breathed deeply into it. The jet fumes were overwhelming. If this were Liberia, she was sure she couldn't live here more than a day.

Trying to appear confident, even when her insides churned and moaned, Ava followed the other passengers into Roberts International Airport. The second she picked up her luggage, men jostled her, asking her if they could help.

The Mercy Ships' staff had already warned her not to trust her bag with any stranger, but rather to bring only what she could carry herself with no problem. She had to be bold to discourage them from asking again and again.

Finally, she made it through customs and to Jessie's familiar blond hair. Jessie was jumping up and down, waving a sign back and forth....as if she needed a sign. And Jessie's dad was there with her. Ava smiled. Her fear vanished. She was safe. She'd reached her destination.

"You're here!" Jessie squeezed her like a long-lost sister, and Mr. Sterling hefted her large suitcase in his strong hands.

"Yes, I am! And I'm so glad to see you guys. You don't even *know* how glad." Ava kept her backpack on as the three made their way out of the airport to one of the ship's land rovers.

Ava felt a freedom that she couldn't define. As soon as she connected with Jessie, her heart lifted, like a feather caught up in a new gust of wind. Ever since that conversation with Michael at Java Cup, she had been on reserve at home and school, afraid to embrace God, and afraid not to, afraid to find out what people would think. So she had kept her thoughts and feelings to herself, terrified that they would spill out like a waterfall.

Her first glimpses of Liberia were mixed with the overwhelming relief of seeing Jessie and her dad as she told them all about her flight, her spring, her graduation—and so her first impressions were only glimpses, much like the preview of a movie. She couldn't very well talk and take everything in all at once.

It was a whirlwind trip from the airport in Monrovia, through the streets of the city, to the port where the ship was docked. United Nations guards, guns at their side, stood watch at the gate to the port.

Once through the secure gate, Ava saw the familiar ship she'd toured just six months earlier. The evening sun had turned the sky deep orange and gray behind the ship. Ava had never seen a sunset so deep and stunning as this one.

Ascending the gangway into the mouth of the ship, Ava was greeted, this time, not as a visitor, but as a volunteer.

A ship briefing awaited her, with paper work to fill out and sign, and jet lag became a reality. Ava's head was spinning.

"We'll take your things to your cabin," Jessie said, "while you fill out all this paperwork. Normally, you would have stayed with us, but since you'll be here six weeks, you've got your own place—kind of."

"Sounds perfect!" Ava tried to sound cheerful in spite of her exhaustion. A feeling of anticipation fluttered in her heart. It was the same way she felt when she was talking to Grandpa Amery at

Christmastime. With time, she had pushed the feeling away, but she could feel something shifting.

"You'll eat dinner in our cabin tonight. And you can even stay there tonight if you want. You can decide," Jessie added. "I'm sure you'll have some early hours in the galley soon."

Always in transition, people came and left the ship on a daily basis. Ava took note of the departure and arrival list posted in the reception area near the gangway. There was her name. *Ava Zinfield.* Yes, she had arrived.

By the time Ava had settled in her cabin, a small room with two bunk beds, a porthole, and a bathroom that connected to another room, it was nearly nine o'clock. Homemade cookies waited for her on top of a bright aqua and blue duvet cover, and a handwritten welcome note from Jessie—and someone named Lydia, from the galley crew. Irene, another galley worker, her soon-to-be roommate, was scheduled to come in two days.

Jessie had talked her through the whole evening and was still chattering away. "And tomorrow is a dress ceremony. You got here just in time. It's the last group of ladies for this outreach."

"Dress ceremony? Oh yes, yes! I remember." Ava recollected the story Jessie had told of the woman who had demanded that the chaplain of Mercy Ships kill her because she didn't want to continue living with her condition and the shame caused by leaking urine.

Jessie stayed while Ava started to unpack her backpack and arrange her belongings on the shelf by her bunk.

"You brought a Bible," Jessie said, smiling.

"Yeah, my grandparents in South Africa sent it to me." Ava smiled. "We have *got* to talk." The flutter in her heart remained, but Ava was determined to hold the tears back until she could talk to Jessie properly.

Ava's suitemates arrived and provided some distraction.

"Hi, Jessie! So this is Ava?" Jasmine asked. "Nice to meet you, Ava. You're from D.C, right?" Jasmine, a 24-year-old nurse, hailed from Mississippi.

"I'm Brittany," said the second suitemate. "And I'm from South Dakota. Welcome." Brittany looked perhaps a bit older, but not much. She was the quieter one. Ava noticed right away that she didn't stay long to chat.

"So how long will you be here?" Jasmine asked.

"Six weeks, and I'm working in the galley. I figured I'd combine my love of cooking and writing, and so here I am," Ava announced with a bit of flair. "I just graduated from high school last week, and now I'm in Africa. It seems so surreal."

"I think we've all experienced that," Jasmine laughed. "We're glad you made it. I'll let you settle in. I've got an early morning tomorrow," she added, retreating into the room she shared with Brittany.

"Hey, come on, Ava," Jessie said. "I'll take you to the Internet café. Don't you want to let your parents know you made it safely?"

"Yes! Good idea." Ava followed Jessie through the ship to the Internet café next to the dining hall.

She sent a short e-mail to her parents letting her know she'd made it, promising more details soon.

Then, she opened another e-mail and began to type:

Hey Michael!

I made it to the ship! I feel a little like Vasco de Gama sailing around the Cape of South Africa, unsure of exactly what lies ahead. Thanks for encouraging me to apply. If it hadn't been for you, I'm not sure that I would have gone through with it. How's Korea? Please write soon! —-Ava

Ava had wanted to say something more, to tell him how much their conversation at Java Cup had meant to her, now that distance safely separated them and she could more freely share her feelings and stay in control. Jessie was waiting, though. And the words she wanted to say just wouldn't form into sentences. It would have to be enough for now.

The girls navigated their way back to Ava's cabin and talked and talked, exchanging travel stories and what-to-expect stories and tell-me-more-about-that-e-mail stories until midnight. There would definitely have to be part two. And three. And four. They would only have two weeks together before Jessie headed back to the States for a month and a half of vacation.

"I'd better let you get some rest," Jessie conceded.

"As much as I hate to admit it, I'm exhausted. I can barely keep my eyes open." Ava had been yawning steadily the last half hour, but Jessie felt somehow like a sister to her—a sister she'd never had.

Nothing felt more comfortable than to put her head on her own pillow after all the traveling, and talking, and adventure.

Silence. She was finally alone. Questions swirled. What would the next six weeks be like? Did she know what she was getting into? What would she say to people who asked her something about God? *What* would people ask? Would she have an answer? After that conversation with Michael at Java Cup on Easter, Ava hadn't talked much about religious things. She purposefully chose to steer the conversation to safer topics around Michael—his grandma's celebration party, the details of her trip, graduation, summer plans.

Ava awoke to a horrendous sound. It felt as if she'd been in bed for only a few minutes. She reached for her watch and a sliver of moonlight from the porthole revealed the time—three o'clock in the morning.

Jumping from bed, disoriented and confused, Ava willed herself to think clearly. A fire alarm? *What did they tell me to do? Where's the lifejacket? I can't remember where to muster. Help! What do I do? God? What's happening?*

Just as she pulled on the life jacket and reached for the cabin door, an announcement came on the public address system. "We apologize for the false alarm. Please disregard. Please disregard." Ava laughed in relief.

She collapsed back into bed until the morning sun woke her gently at 8 A.M Normally, she would have been scheduled for a tour, but she'd already had her own personal tour of the ship in South Africa just six months ago.

At nine, the dress ceremony would begin. She didn't have much time to dress and study the ship's map before heading up to the galley to meet Jessie for breakfast. When would they have time for part two? Ava hadn't yet told Jessie about the pearls. Or the dream.

CHAPTER 23

Jessie led Ava through the corridors of the ship and down a few stairwells to the hospital ward. Once through the double doors, Ava gasped. Six months ago, she had seen this very ward, empty and waiting for people desperate for medical attention. And now, she witnessed in real life the vision of Mercy Ships, to bring hope and healing to the poor. Patients filled the beds.

The nurse at the ward entrance recognized Jessie right away, "Hey, girl! You've brought your friend to watch a dress ceremony, have you? My name is Martina. And you're Ava, right? I heard you'd be coming."

"Uhm, yes. Nice to meet you!" Had she come across as too excited? Too nervous?

"Where's *she* from?" Ava lightly elbowed Jessie. The question had become a common one as they made their way around the ship.

"She's from Sweden," Jessie told her. "Now come on, let's find a place to sit. I think they're about to get started."

The ward bustled with nurses in their scrubs, patients in their gowns, and crew members in their blue jeans, but four women stood out above all the joyful commotion. In regal African dress, Ava saw the first woman whispering to and laughing with one of the nurses. She wore a dress the color of sand, woven with patterns of sea green and burgundy *S* shapes. Circling her neck, seven yellow-gold flowers with intricate white centers formed a smile at the top of her dress as big as the smile she wore on her face. On her head, the traditional African head piece, made of the same material as the dress, seemed to crown the young woman an African princess.

The laughing nurse leaned in slightly to the woman and lightly brushed her cheeks with a final few touches of powder. She managed to apply lipstick in between the girlish giggles of the African princess before her, and when she finished, the woman's lips glowed like a burnished copper penny in the sun. *Such a beautiful young woman,* Ava thought. *I wonder what her story is.*

As Ava began to observe the rest of the group assembled in the ward, it felt as if twenty pairs of eyes were noticing her one by one, and the common theme was kindness and acceptance.

Ava felt relieved and followed Jessie through the ward past two tall blue and white drums. An African lady wearing a dress of yellow, red, and white squares on black and white polka dot print sat behind them, waiting and smiling. She looked right at Ava and smiled a very warm smile of welcome.

"Attention everyone, we'll be getting started now. Find a place and let us celebrate these women who have a new life ahead of them. The first woman to tell her story is Yah. Yah, come."

The African princess stepped forward, somewhat shyly. The smiling nurse encouraged her with a hug and whispered something in her ear.

"My story..."

"Amen!" a nurse shouted.

"My story begins two years ago. I was fourteen."

Ava and Jessie turned to each other simultaneously, eyes wide. *Fourteen.* Ava had thought she was at least an older teen, maybe even in her twenties.

"Yes, I was fourteen. I found out I was pregnant. I was happy, but I was scared. I was not married. But I loved my boyfriend very much, and he loved me. When it came time to have the baby, the only place to go was the bush. So I went alone. I would have the baby. I would be a good mama."

Ava strained to understand the unfamiliar Liberian accent, but she didn't miss a word.

"But I felt trouble right away. And after the first day, the baby did not come. I was in much pain. So much pain. I wondered if this was normal. Then the next day, still the baby didn't come. I was very worried. I was so afraid."

"After two days, a man came to help me. He said he knew how to help. But after he tried and tried to deliver my baby, he said, 'I can't.' My stomach was swollen. My tears were all gone. Finally, two old women came to help me. They tried to deliver my baby, but my baby was already dead."

The woman's voice grew stronger and yet more fragile as it swelled with the terrifying memories of those days in the bush.

"I picked myself up. The ladies helped me back to the village. That night I slept and slept. I was exhausted. But when I woke up, my bed was wet. I didn't know what was wrong. I thought it was normal. But I couldn't control it. The next day, the next day. The same thing."

"I tried to go back to school. I tried to sit by my friends, but they say, 'Pee, pee, smelly.' And they laughed at me. They did not want me around. So I stopped going to school. My boyfriend left me. He knew I could not have children. I was so alone. I was so afraid. I did not know anyone who had my problem." Tears fell freely from her watery, bright eyes.

Ava realized she had been biting her bottom lip. She had never imagined that someone so young would have to endure such a heart-wrenching trauma.

"Then one day, I was in church…" the young girl said.

"Hallelujah! Praise the Lord!" The same nurse who had shouted *Amen* shouted out another proclamation which caused the entire ward to break into applause and cheers. The African princess wiped a tear from her eye and broke into a wide, wide smile.

Ava took a deep breath. She'd been listening so intently, she'd barely even been breathing.

"I was in church and someone told me they heard on the radio about a ship," the young girl continued. "The people on the ship could help me, they said. I just needed to get there. But I had no money. My family had no money. My father was killed in the war. My brother was killed in the war."

"I was telling God, *thank you, thank you, thank you. Please help me get to the ship. Please, God, hear my prayer. Please, God.*"

"My church collected an offering. It was enough to get me to the next town by taxi. I had to go alone. I was so afraid. In the next town,

I found a job washing clothes, and after two weeks, I had enough money to come here to Monrovia."

Ava felt the familiar ache in her throat as Yah continued her story. "I was very scared to enter the ship. I had never seen a ship before. I had never been to see the ocean. It was *so BIG*. But the nurses were so nice. I met three other women that day with my same problem. I had no idea. I thought I was alone. We were all having surgery the same day."

"The first moment I awoke from surgery, I saw the nurses beside me. Shari was by my side. She said everything went fine. And I was feeling weak, but I knew in my heart everything was fine now."

Suddenly, the lady sitting behind the tall blue and white drums began beating out a rhythm. Yah began to sing her words of thanks to the beat of the drums, to the shake of the maracas.

"I just want to praise God! I praise the God who formed me in the womb. He knows all my trouble. He helped me when I cried to him. Thank you, God, Thank you, Jesus! Thank you to the Mercy Ship. Thank you to the nurses. Thank you, God!"

The lady behind the blue and white drums began to sing. The people echoed her.

Ava watched the young woman praising God, tears still wet on her face.

This is the kind of woman who could break and pour out an expensive jar of perfume on Jesus' feet. After all, she has good reason. What reason do I have? Would I even do it? Could I? Could I do it in front of my family, as Mary had done, as these women are doing? What exactly would I say?

Ava sensed that any minute, someone might ask her something about God that she would not be able to answer. She'd overheard one crew member ask another at breakfast, "So how did God bring you here to the ship?"

Did God bring me to this ship? Or did I choose to come? Good question. Ava laughed at her own thoughts. She'd be sure to e-mail Michael and ask him what he thought.

For the rest of the dress ceremony, Ava felt her heart beating in rhythm with every woman's story, as if she were hearing a song for the first time, or the thousandth time. Was she herself a Christian? Had she been believing in God since Easter? How could she know for sure? It seemed to her that believing in God was more like writing an essay rather than solving an equation. It was personal. She needed to explore for herself—to write and erase and think and write again. But then again, it didn't feel as if she were the only one writing.

CHAPTER 24

Ship paperwork behind her and a Saturday free before her, Ava jumped in the land rover with Jessie and the team who were headed out to the Aged and Abandoned Orphanage for their weekly visit. Ava wanted to soak everything in, especially this day, when she'd get to meet the children that would benefit from the new dorms being constructed for which she and Michael had helped raise money.

The land rover bumped through the pot-holed streets of Monrovia. In the intersections, instead of stoplights, Ava saw men directing the traffic. A taxi cab, filled with at least ten people sitting on top of one another in random fashion, swerved past the group from Mercy Ships. The trunk was bulging with all kinds of trappings and tied with rope to keep the precious cargo from falling out.

At an intersection in the heart of the city, a little boy about six years old held out two bags of water—two clear plastic bags of water the size of a sandwich bag. *Water for sale in a bag in the middle of the street?* Another girl held out a box of Chic-lets gum and pleaded with the passengers in the land rover to please buy some. Ava wished she could stop and buy every last piece so that the girl could go play.

The ride to the orphanage took about thirty minutes from the ship. Ava pressed her face to the window, peering this time, for real, right into the heart of Africa. Their vehicle turned at the intersection and bounced down one of the dirt roads deeper into a world in stark contrast to her upscale D.C. lifestyle.

Here she was, passing right through the lives of these people living on less than a dollar a day. Modern conveniences didn't seem to exist. The dwellings of the people were made of gray cinder blocks with porches of tin propped up by branches or skinny tree saplings. One structure had walls made of translucent plastic, no door, and only a crude window carefully constructed in the plastic sheeting.

The ground around the houses, Ava noted, consisted of gray dirt, void of any grass, but splashes of color punctuated the landscape. A woman in a bright turquoise skirt and white tank top stopped to stare, a huge tray of something resembling dried fish on her head. Bright green and yellow buckets and tubs, set out in the yards for washing and bathing, brightened the poverty. A mother and her children rested on top of a green blanket spread out on the gray dirt under the shade of a big tree with bright green leaves. A pair of neon-orange flip flops, the standard shoe of the city, rested haphazardly nearby.

Two women walked side by side, dressed in formal-looking African dresses, complete with headdresses to match—one in sky blue, the other in bright pink with varied patterns. Behind them, the buildings seemed to crumble, but the women walked tall and proud.

Three young men then passed into Ava's view wearing Western clothes—baggy jean shorts and loose-fitting tank tops and T-shirts. Ava knew from her research that almost no one had jobs. Eighty percent of the people were unemployed. A general listlessness had settled in the hearts of the people. The war was over, and they were ready to move on.

Young men sat on their porches, talking and laughing. Families set out small wooden tables filled with dried plantain chips, peanuts, mangos, or popcorn. Whatever they had, they sold. Clothing hung out to dry, sometimes stretched between two houses. Life zoomed by, yet stayed perfectly still.

The team in the land rover had been talking about the orphanage kids and the plan for the day. Ava had been content to stare out the window and listen, until one of the team members addressed her.

"So, Ava, are you excited?" Marie asked her, after the team leader had finished briefing the team on the plans for the day. Marie was from Miami, Ava had learned when they'd all introduced themselves to her as they met on the dock to load up for the trip to the orphanage. They'd all held hands and prayed, and Ava, never having done that, found herself, eyes open, peeking around the circle.

"Very excited," Ava told her. "A friend of mine and I helped raise money for the kids at the orphanage, and I'm so glad I can finally meet them. Jessie even sent me a video when you guys came at Easter, and so I feel like I already know some of the kids."

"So Jessie told us how she met you on Boulder's Beach in South Africa. Isn't it amazing how God just brings things together like that?" Marie asked her.

Ava's heart was bursting. Of course it was, wasn't it? "Yes, I never would have imagined," she told the group, who were now all listening.

Ava wondered how much Jessie had shared with the group. Had she told them that her friend was an atheist, and at most, skeptical that God existed? Did the team think she had become a Christian? Hadn't she?

Ava began to wish she'd talked things through a bit more with Michael. He surely would have explained more, shared more, helped her more before she came halfway across the world to work on a Christian ship. But she hadn't been ready.

A little boy, squatting beside a house, suddenly leapt forward and began running full speed alongside the land rover, waving with both hands as his nimble, bare feet carried him down the dirt path beside the road. For fifteen seconds of his life, he ran and smiled. Perhaps he did that every day. Or did he just do that when the land rover from the *Mercy Ship* passed by each Saturday on its way to the orphanage?

"Look at that little boy!" Ava beamed. "He looks so happy!" She was glad for the distraction from having to say anything more to the team.

"Yes, these children always have the most beautiful smiles," Marie added.

A few more minutes down the dirt road and Jessie announced, "We're here! Just love on the kids. They'll love you right back. That's pretty much all you need to know."

As soon as Ava and the orphanage team stepped out of the land rover, children of all sizes surrounded them with beaming smiles, reaching for the soccer balls and hula hoops the crew had brought for them to play with.

Mr. McKenzie, the team leader, directed the high school students to spread the blue, twenty-foot tarp out beneath the palm-like trees. There was no grass in the big yard next to the orphanage. The children's constant running all over the yard never gave it a chance to grow.

Some of the boys ran after Jacob, the Texan boy, as he led them in a game of soccer. Here beneath the sun and shade of Africa at the orphanage, the only rule seemed to be, have fun. Mrs. Landers, the assistant principal from the academy, pulled out a large parachute that vibrated with the rhythm of Africa in greens, reds, yellows, and blues.

"On the count of three, lift!" she shouted. The parachute launched into the air and the children squealed with delight, just as they might do anywhere in the world. "Greens and blues switch places," she commanded, and children scurried to find a place on another piece of the parachute. Ava ducked under with them and mixed right in with the fray of laughing children.

On the blue tarp, a handful of children crowded around two crew members with long hair. They much preferred to take this opportunity to braid the smooth, fine hair of these white girls visiting their village, their home.

"The first time we came," said Jessie, "a little girl was so afraid of us that she started crying. She had never seen a white person before."

After the parachute games, Ava held one end of a long jump rope while Jessie held the other. They must have spun their arms a few hundred times, listening to the children chant songs and jump until they fell over in a piles of giggles.

Soon, it was time to gather on the blue tarp for the Bible story.

"Listen up, everyone! I have someone very special to introduce to you today." Jessie hollered over the squeals of the children.

Ava stood at the front with Jessie. Some of the children had already met her, but this was her official introduction.

"Everyone, this is Ava, our newest team member!" Jessie announced. "She'll be coming out to visit you for several weeks while she's here working on the ship. We waved to her in the video, remember?"

The children clapped and almost in unison said, "Hello, Ava!"

Ava found a seat on the tarp, and a child immediately crawled on her lap, as if she'd known Ava forever.

"What is your name?" Ava asked her. The little girl had been one jumping rope with Ava and Jessie, but with the blur of children jumping in and out of the rope, Ava hadn't asked her for her name then.

"Jo Jo," the little girl answered.

Ava instantly recognized her. Jo Jo! She was the little leader in the video who had led the children in singing. And she was the little girl who'd opened the first egg, with the palm branches. That was how the story with the Easter eggs had begun. Jesus had entered Jerusalem and the people had waved palm branches, excited that Jesus was coming to town. They would have a king at last, Mrs. Landers had said.

As Ava sat on the tarp with little Jo Jo and the other children, she gazed into the bright blue African sky. The Bible story today was about a disciple named Peter who went back to fishing after Jesus had died on the cross. He and his friends had fished all night and caught nothing. Nothing at all. But then a man had shown up early in the morning and called from the shore, "Cast your nets on the other side of the boat!"

And so the men did as the man on the shore had told them. Immediately, they caught fish—so many that they could barely haul them in. Ava listened, hoping for answers of her own.

Almost instantly, one of the disciples said, "It's Jesus!"

When Peter realized that it was indeed Jesus, he jumped into the water and swam about a hundred yards to the shore. The other disciples followed in the boat, towing the net full of fish because they couldn't haul them into the boat.

Ava considered the story and thought about her own life. She felt exactly like Peter. She wanted to jump into the water and swim toward Jesus. If only she could!

Ava stored up the pieces of the story in her heart. It was the *third* time Jesus had appeared to his disciples after he was resurrected. Once, he seemed to know, was not enough.

"Let's stand up, now," Mrs. Landers encouraged the children, "and sing!"

Little Jo Jo stepped forward, appearing timid, yet full of confidence. Her small body sure had a big voice. She sang the first words of the song, and the children echoed her, clapping between the phrases.

"Now I believe today!" she sang.

"Now I believe today!" the children repeated.

"Jesus has set me free!" she continued.

"Jesus has set me free!" the group repeated, clapping.

Ava felt a tug on her hand, and looking down, her eyes met those of a little boy.

"Why....," he said, but Ava couldn't hear the rest.

She leaned down and put her ear to his mouth. "What did you ask?"

"Why aren't you singing?" he asked her.

Ava looked into the little boy's chocolate eyes, just like her own. "I'm not sure. But I will sing! I *will...*"

And Ava sang. As she echoed little Jo Jo's strong and sure voice, freedom burst forth from her heart as she declared with her mouth that she believed. It was an indescribable joy.

* * *

That night, before Ava slipped into her bunk on the Mercy Ship *Anastasis* docked in Monrovia, Liberia, she remembered what Jessie had written her in one of her e-mails. Quietly, she knelt beside her bed and purposefully tried to bring to mind all the times God had tried to get through to her. It seemed so clear now. The trail, Michael, Jessie, the rainbow, the pearls, the Valentine, her grandparents and the sea-colored Bible, the flyer on the bulletin board about the Easter service, and the little African boy who asked her, "Why aren't you singing?" A simple prayer formed on her lips, and peace like she'd never known enveloped her.

She knew in her heart it was time to write to Michael and pick up where they had left off at Java Cup. She couldn't find the words then, but now, as she reached for her pearl necklace, she knew exactly what she would say.

DISCUSSION GUIDE

Each question correlates with the same chapter in the book.

1. Do you think there is a lot of pressure to have a boyfriend or girlfriend in your circle of friends? What are the benefits of just being friends with guys during high school?

2. Have you ever been invited to a Christian meeting or church service? Did you go? What was the experience like?

3. Why do you think people would say, "Just be good for goodness' sake?

4. Have you ever met or reconnected with family that you hadn't seen in a long time? Did you feel as though you had to "make up for lost time?" Describe your experience.

5. Describe a gift you received that meant a great deal to you.

6. Take a few minutes to look at Mercy Ships' website at www.mercy-ships.org. Click on the "stories" link and read a patient's story. How does this story impact you?

7. What is your experience with prayer? How has God answered prayer in your own life? Does he sometimes say "no" to things that are extremely important to us?

8. Are you more like Ava or Jessie? Or are you somewhere in between? Explain.

9. What parts of the Bible have you read? Do you have any questions you want to ask about it? Do you believe the Bible is relevant for today?

10. What does your name mean? How do you think Ava felt, sitting in the church service with her family?

11. Do you believe, like Miranda, that Christians have no fun?

12. Describe a time when you were moved to help someone less fortunate than you.

13. Do you believe God created the world? Or are things just here by chance?

14. Have you ever sensed that God was speaking to you? How can we know? Tell about this experience.

15. Has there been someone in your life who has pointed you to God? Tell about that person and how he/she has influenced you.

16. Have you ever gotten a job and tried to save money for something you really wanted?

17. Do you think you know what it means to have a relationship with God?

18. Share how you became a Christian. Note: God works in each person's life uniquely. Your experience may be nothing like Ava's.

19. Do you ever feel like Sarah? Forced to go to church and not really seeing the point?

20. What does Easter mean to you?

21. Do you and your friends ever talk about spiritual things? Why or why not?

22. Will Ava share what she's experienced with her family?

23. Have you ever felt discouraged, thinking God has stopped caring for you? How do we make it through the times when God seems silent?

24. What do you think Ava's prayer is at the end of the book?

Please e-mail the author at <u>pearls4ava@gmail.com</u> to ask questions or share answers to any questions above. She would love to have a conversation with you! You can also visit the Facebook page, "Pearls on a Broken String."

ABOUT THE AUTHOR

Valerie Cox currently teaches high school English in her hometown of Cleveland, Texas. In 2005-2006, she served as a volunteer fifth and sixth grade teacher onboard the Mercy Ship Anastasis. This book was inspired by her experiences in Cape Town, where she joined the ship, and in Liberia, where the crew spent seven months serving the people of West Africa. To contact the author, please write to pearls4ava@ gmail.com or visit the Facebook page "Pearls on a Broken String." She would LOVE to hear from you!

ACKNOWLEDGMENTS

To my college classmates from East Texas Baptist University who honored me with the "Future Famous Author" award in 1998---thank you for the vote of confidence! A very special thank you to my two instructors from The Institute of Children's Literature---Jan Czech and Clara Gillow Clark---whose advice and unfailing support helped make my dream of writing this book a reality. Thank you to each family member and friend who kept hearing about this book and always believed that I would finish it someday! Much appreciation to numerous friends who have encouraged me in this process and to the handful who were kind enough to read a draft of my book and offer encouragement and suggestions: Rebecca Cheng, Yashira Ortiz, Mike Rule, Nancy Patrick, "Wolf", Mandi Lizotte, Paul Robinson, and my mom, Shirley Cox. I am also deeply indebted to Diane Rickard with Mercy Ships International Media Relations who also read my manuscript and offered support and advice. An extra special thank you to my sister Lanette Sikes who let me borrow her camera to snap a photo of my niece Jordan Cox for the front cover and to Alice Salinas who convinced me I could take a great picture. Thank you, Jordan, for being such a willing and amiable model—and an amazing niece!

Thank you ultimately to my Creator and Redeemer, Jesus Christ, who enables me to write my story.

His divine power has given us everything we need for a godly life through our knowledge of him who called us by his own glory and goodness. 2 Peter 1: 3